DARK DAY

DARK DAY

BRANDON HALL SERIES BOOK 3

MIKE RYAN

WWW.MIKERYANBOOKS.COM

Copyright © 2020 by Mike Ryan

All rights reserved.

No part of this book may be reproduced in any form or by any electronic or mechanical means, including information storage and retrieval systems, without written permission from the author, except for the use of brief quotations in a book review.

Cover By: Warren Dezign

Edited By: Anna Albo

1

Hall was working on his first official case after getting his private investigator's license. It was a small job, following a man around to find out if he was cheating on his wife. The wife hired Hall a week ago, and he'd been following the husband around since then. Hall had heard from some other PIs that these kinds of cases were the worst, but he didn't realize it himself until he was on it. It was extremely boring following a guy around on his extracurricular activities, taking pictures and showing them to his wife later. But it was his first official case, and it was a paying job, so it was better than nothing. Once he was in the business for a while, he could and would probably be more selective with the jobs that he accepted. But for now, money was money, and he needed all that he could.

Charlotte was still working from home, but she

hoped to help Hall as much as she could. It was more exciting than design work. But until the business was up and running and making more money, the bills had to be paid somehow. They were hoping to eventually have a separate office they could conduct business in, but for now, they had to use the apartment. So if they needed to meet any clients, they would have to use nearby coffee houses and diners. They didn't want to be parading people through their apartment, especially if they had clients that weren't the most trustworthy.

They bought a big L-shaped desk that they put in the corner of the living room, so each of them had a separate workspace for now. It was getting close to dinner time and Charlotte had just finished her work for the day. Hall walked in the door just as she was turning her computer off. She gave him a kiss as he came over to the desk and sat down at his computer. He plugged his phone in to upload some pictures. He then removed a notebook from the drawer and started making some notes.

"How'd it go today?"

"Oh, you know, just the usual," Hall said dejectedly.

"What's the matter?"

"I hate doing stuff like this. People told me how boring it would be. But I didn't realize *how* boring it would be. I mean, it is the worst."

"You know every case isn't going to be exciting and super important."

"Yeah, I know, but I dunno, it's just... different. I didn't mind actually helping people and investigating things. I feel like I'm good at that, you know? With this, though, it feels like anybody could do it."

"Well, it's important to the person who hired you."

"Yeah, I know, and I'm not trying to trivialize her problems or anything, it's just..."

"It's not like investigating a murder."

"Yeah, it's definitely not."

"I guess you have to look at the alternative and what else you could be doing."

"I could be starting my own trucking business and trying to get that off the ground, that's what I could be doing."

"Would you really like that more?"

Hall shrugged. "I don't know. This doesn't even feel like work. It feels like spying."

"Some things are going to be exciting. Some things are going to be dull. It's just the way it is."

"I'm just not sure this is what I want to be doing."

"Brandon, you did all that work to get your license and now you're gonna give up after one case?"

"I didn't say I was giving up. Not yet. I'm just not sure I want to do... this."

"You can tailor the business to what you want. More investigative work, security, things like that."

As Hall flipped through a few pages of his notebook, Charlotte noticed the name Rankin scribbled on a few of the pages.

"Are you still looking for him?" Charlotte asked.

"Who?"

"Rankin. I noticed his name written down a few times."

Hall shrugged. "I dunno. Not really. I was trying to see if I could figure out who he really was. Just something to pass some of my other spare time. You know, when I'm not out taking pictures of people."

"I think you need to cross his name out and forget about him. The police don't know who he is, you're not gonna be able to figure it out from here, and that case is dead anyway. Probably shouldn't use those words since some of the people were literally dead, but... it's solved."

"I don't know. It kind of bothers me that this guy is still out there, pulling the strings, making everyone else pay for his stuff, and he gets off scot-free."

"Some people are just smart enough to get away with it."

"But they shouldn't be. He should pay for the things he's done."

"Brandon, forget him. He's a ghost now. He always was. Rankin's probably not even his real name. Just concentrate on what you're doing."

Hall looked at the screen, observing a picture of his target kissing another woman who was not his wife. "Concentrate on what I'm doing, huh?" Hall then looked at his beautiful girlfriend.

"OK, so not literally. And this is basically wrapped up anyway, isn't it? I mean, you've got the proof, right?"

"Well, yeah, kind of."

"What do you mean, kind of? I see the proof right there."

"Well, the wife wanted me to follow him for a week. It's only been six days. Got one more to go."

"Oh."

"And this is only number three."

"What do you mean, number three?"

"This is the third different woman I've photographed with this guy this week," Hall said.

"Three?! Man, he's busy."

"And what's even worse is he's taken all three to the same restaurant for dinner."

"He's got no shame," Charlotte said. "Guess he doesn't care if people recognize him. Hope he doesn't take his wife to the same place."

"He doesn't. I asked her about it, and she said she's never been there."

"So she knows?"

"She knows he's cheating. She just wanted proof."

"See? You're helping to change people's lives."

Hall looked at her, then the two shared a laugh. It wasn't quite the definition he had in mind when he thought of helping people.

"How's this guy get away with having dinner with all these people?" Charlotte asked. "What's his wife doing?"

"Oh, she works nights at a hospital."

"Oh, nice. She's helping people for real, and her turd of a husband is out playing Don Juan. Nice."

"There's somebody for everybody, right?"

"Unfortunately, it seems so. Some people don't deserve anybody, though. Anyway, enough about that. So what do you say we go out after dinner?"

"That's nice, but I can't," Hall said. "Gotta follow this guy again."

"I thought you already did that."

"These are from last night."

"What were you doing earlier?"

"Trying to get more business. Talked to a few companies about working for them, dropped off some business cards, things like that."

"Oh. Any luck?"

"A few said they were interested. They had to kick it around a little first. I dunno, we'll see."

Charlotte gave him a kiss on the cheek. "I'm sure at least one of them will hire you."

"We'll see."

"About later, do you really need to follow this guy again? I mean, how much proof do you need? You've already got the goods on him. What good is following him another night?"

"Well, the wife asked me to follow him every night and gave me a little extra to do it, so I really should."

Charlotte looked at him seductively. "Are you sure there's nothing I can do to change your mind?"

"Uh..." Hall flicked his eyes and looked away, not wanting to get sucked into her charms. "So is dinner ready?"

"Depends on what you want."

"Just something quick and easy."

"Quick and easy, huh? Just the way you like it."

Hall smiled. "Uh... I refuse to answer on the grounds I may incriminate myself."

"Smart man."

They went into the kitchen and made ham and cheese sandwiches and some chips, then tried to talk about something other than Hall's work. Somehow, the conversation seemed to come back to it, though. Once the time hit seven o'clock, Hall knew he had to go.

"What are you gonna do if he already left?"

"He hasn't," Hall answered. "This is the sixth day I've been on this guy. He's had the same pattern the last five days. He leaves at seven thirty, then meets his date at the restaurant, then goes back to their place, then goes home before his wife gets there at midnight."

"Seems he needs a new pattern."

"Think he needs a new brain, but at least this guy is predictable. Makes it easier for me."

"Who knows, maybe you'll get lucky and get thrown into a more interesting case while you're out there?"

"This ain't the movies. I doubt something like that will happen."

"Never know. You could be one of those people

who somehow gets drawn into things. Or they're drawn to you, I guess."

"Yeah, I don't think that's gonna happen here. This guy's not wrapped into anything other than other women. And that's enough."

Hall gathered his things and went to the door. Before he left, Charlotte went over and gave him a kiss and a hug.

"I'll wait up for you. Unless you'll be too tired and wanna go straight to bed."

"I doubt I'll be that tired," Hall replied. "I'll just be sitting there. It's not like anything interesting is gonna happen."

"Well, I'll say a little prayer that you get some more action."

"Thanks. I doubt that prayer's gonna be at the top of anyone's list to answer, though."

"It's the thought that counts."

"It is. But there's nothing that's gonna make this night more interesting. Nothing."

2

For most of the night, Hall was right. It was just another boring night in a long string of them. Nothing new or interesting. His client's husband did just as he did all the other nights. He ate at the restaurant with a different woman, then went back to her place for a nightcap. This woman was a little more upscale than the others, though, at least by outside appearances. The other three lived in either apartments or modest-sized homes. The woman tonight lived in what looked like an upper echelon house. Judging by the neighborhood, Hall doubted any house would list for under a million dollars. Lush green grass, plenty of yard space, two- and three-car garages, and at least three thousand square feet to go along with all the upscale finishes that the neighborhood provided.

There were no private gates around the complex or

any of the homes, so Hall was able to park across the street from the house, in front of one of the woman's neighbors. He figured he'd stay for an hour or so, get some pictures, then take off. He didn't want to stay too long and risk somebody calling the cops on him, wary of him hanging around for so long. Not that he was afraid of the cops showing up, but there was no reason to butt heads with them already. He'd save that for a more important case.

Hall was watching the upstairs bedroom window, where he'd seen the two people walk back and forth in front of it. Through his camera, he saw the man without a shirt, and the woman in only a bra. This was the first time he'd actually seen them since they'd first arrived, so he figured they were finishing up their activities. Hall took a few more pictures, wanting to get out of there before the man came out of the house.

Before starting up his car, Hall looked through the window one final time. He took a few more pictures, then was stunned to see a third person appear in the frame of the window. He couldn't believe what he saw next. The man had a gun in his hand and held it in front of him, in plain view of the window. Hall took a few more pictures, though he couldn't see anyone other than the man with the gun at the moment. A few seconds later, Hall heard several shots fired. Hall quickly got on the phone to call it in.

"Nine-one-one, what is your emergency?"

"Shots fired, 1612 Southern Street, not sure about

Dark Day

victims, looked like one shooter. Get Detective Bradham over here now, and tell him Brandon Hall is already on scene. Going inside to check it out now."

"Hold on, sir…"

Hall didn't hold on, though. He didn't know what was going on, but he assumed the people inside were dead or badly injured. And they couldn't afford to wait for help to arrive. He was the help. If they weren't dead, the shooter could easily finish them off while waiting for the police to arrive. There was nothing else Hall could do, in his mind, except barge in and do what he could.

He went over to the front door and tried to open it, but it was locked. He didn't have time to jiggle with it or try to bust it open, so he went over to the window. He looked down at the ground and saw a couple of tiny rocks and smashed the window with them. A couple pieces of glass broke, one of which cut Hall on the arm. He wasn't really worried about that, though. He just had to get in there. He reached through the broken part of the window and unlocked it, then slid the window up and climbed through.

Once inside, he immediately looked for the stairs and headed for them. Just as he got to the bottom of the steps, he looked up and saw a man at the top of the stairs, pointing a gun at him. The man fired just as Hall dove out of the way. The man then rushed down the stairs as Hall got back to his feet. The man pointed his gun at Hall again, but Hall knocked it out of his hand before he had a chance to fire. They struggled for a few moments, then Hall felt a knee pushing into his stomach, causing him to hunch over a little. That was all the other man needed to get the upper hand in the conflict. He then gave Hall what felt like a few karate chops, one of which was to the back of his neck. Hall fell to the ground, giving the man ample opportunity to get away.

The man didn't try to go for his gun again. He was just thankful that he was going to be able to get out of there. He raced out of the house as Hall slowly got back to his feet, holding the back of his head. Hall saw the man run to the back of the house and took off after him. Hall rushed into the kitchen and saw the back door open and went over to it. He looked out, but didn't see a sign of the man anywhere. He'd gotten away.

Hall sighed, frustrated that he let the man get the better of him. But on the bright side, at least he hadn't been shot in the process of tangling with the man. Hall left the door open, careful not to touch it in case there were fingerprints on it. He walked back to the stairs and stepped over the gun, once again not wanting to touch it. Hall rushed up the steps and looked in a couple of the rooms to make sure no one was there. He then found the bedroom the two bodies were in. And they were dead.

As Hall walked closer to the bodies on the floor, both lying next to each other, he could see the similarity in which they were shot. They had one bullet in their foreheads and another in their chests. Exact same placement. Whoever did this was a pro. An amateur would not have been that precise. Hall stood there for a moment, looking at them, thinking about how terrible it all was. For the past week he'd been thinking about what a creep this guy was, and now he ended up dead. Hall figured he was already going to have a hard-enough time telling the man's wife about his activities, and now she'd have to hear about his death. Well, the police would do that. At least he didn't have to take care of that part, though he'd still have to talk to her about what he knew.

Hall looked around the room briefly, trying to see if he could come up with any clues, though he was careful not to touch anything. He was looking to see if anything was out in plain sight. He definitely wasn't going to add his fingerprints to the crime scene. With nothing jumping out at him, he went back downstairs and waited outside for the police to show up. A patrol car came by only a minute later, quickly followed by another one.

Hall explained the situation to the officers on scene, then gave a detailed account of everything he did up to that point. They asked him to wait there while they checked the inside of the house and for the detectives to show up, which Hall was planning on doing anyway. As he waited for Bradham to appear, he called Charlotte.

"Hey, how's it going?"

"Uh, good, I guess," Hall answered. "I just wanted to let you know I might be a little late tonight."

"What? Why? You really have to keep following that creep all night?"

"Um, well, no, you see... the creep is dead."

Charlotte was briefly silent. "What?"

"Yeah, the creep is dead."

"How? What happened?"

"I was taking pictures of him at this woman's house, then all of a sudden this guy shows up out of nowhere and shoots them both."

"Oh, wow. That's crazy."

"I know."

"When I said I'd hoped things would get more interesting, I really didn't mean it. Not like that."

"I know."

"Are the police there?"

"Yeah, they're here now. I guess I have to give them my story about the shooter since I saw him and all. Seems like a tough guy. My neck still hurts."

"What?"

Hall realized what he said and tried to backpedal. "Nothing."

"What did you say?"

"Uh, it was nothing really."

"Did you get into a confrontation with this guy?"

"Uh, well, I mean, since I saw the thing happen, I went in there and tried to help. That's all."

"And you went in there, knowing there was a man with a gun? Are you crazy?"

"Charlotte, I didn't know if the people were dead or not. I was just trying to help."

"And go up against a guy who had a gun?! Once again, are you crazy?!"

"It was nothing."

"Nothing?! You're lucky he didn't shoot you too."

"Well, he tried. I ducked out of the way."

"Oh my god, you're gonna kill me. Are you OK?"

"Yeah, he just chopped the back of my neck with his hand. Felt like he hit me with a brick or something," Hall said.

"Well, that's saying something considering what you can do. You're just lucky you're not more seriously hurt."

"I'm fine."

"Yeah, no thanks to you. Am I gonna have to go out with you on every job from now on just to make sure you don't do something stupid?"

"I didn't do anything stupid."

"Says you."

"Oh, look, Bradham's here. Looks like I'm gonna have to go."

"You know darn well we're gonna have another talk about this later, right?"

Hall sighed, knowing that was true. "Yeah, yeah."

"Is Bradham really there, or are you just trying to get off the hook?"

"Um, yeah, there he is now. Listen, I'll call you when I'm done here and on the way home, OK?"

"OK. Be safe."

"Everything's over. There's nothing to be safe about."

"Knowing you, Brandon, you'd find a way."

Hall nodded, even though she couldn't see him. Unfortunately, that last part was probably also true. He did seem to have a knack for finding trouble. Hall put his phone back in his pocket and leaned up against a patrol car as Detective Bradham walked over to him.

"You mind telling me what this is all about?"

Hall looked confused. "Uh, two people got killed."

"I know that part. I heard. You mind telling me how you just stumbled upon it?"

"I was following this guy, Jesse Armstrong, now deceased, because his wife thought he was cheating on her."

"And you just happened to catch a murder at the same time?"

"Well, I've been following him all week."

"You got your license yet?"

Hall showed it to him. "Freshly printed."

"Great. Now I'll have you up in my ass all the time."

"You sound so friendly when you talk like that."

"This is the second murder I've had in three days, so excuse me if my mood isn't the greatest."

"What was the first one?"

"How 'bout you tell me about this one first?"

"I thought you already heard," Hall said.

"I'd like to hear it from you since you saw it live."

Hall relayed his story again, just as he'd told it to the first officer he'd encountered. He might have given a few extra details since he knew Bradham so well.

"So you got a picture of this guy?"

Hall took out his phone and showed the pictures he took. Bradham looked at them, studying the picture of the killer the most.

"Not really a clear shot of his face. It's kind of to the side."

"Well, sorry I couldn't get a full close-up," Hall replied. "He was kind of busy at the time."

Bradham handed the phone back. "You'll have to come downtown so we can grab those pictures for evidence."

"I figured as much."

"I heard you tangled with the guy too?"

"Yeah. Like I said, he shot at me, then we wrestled around a bit."

Bradham shook his head in a mocking fashion. "I didn't think I'd see the day when someone was able to take you out."

"He got in a lucky shot."

"Uh huh. I'll want you to look at the mug book too, to see if you can identify this guy. And if that fails, then we'll bring in a sketch artist."

"OK."

"What'd he look like again?"

Hall showed him the picture he took, then described him as well. Bradham studied the photo one more time. "Could be the same guy."

"What guy?"

"Same guy as the other day. Maybe. Physical description matches. Same MO too. Two shots. One to the head, and the other to the chest."

"How many victims were in that one?"

"Just one." Bradham then looked at the house. "Well, I better go in there and check it out. You stay here until I get out."

"Can't I just go up with you?"

"I can't have civilians messing around in a crime scene."

"I'm not a civilian."

"Non-authorized police personnel. Is that better?"

"Not really."

"That'd be just what I needed, a case getting kicked out of court because they contend you were in there screwing around, touching stuff, messing up the evidence."

"You know I wouldn't do that."

"I know. Just humor me."

"I'll wear gloves if you want."

"Just do me a favor and listen to me for once," Bradham said. "Sit in the car, play some solitaire on your phone, and I'll be back in a little bit. Then we can go back to the station."

"Can I play blackjack instead?"

Bradham gave him a mocking smile, then walked away, going toward the house. Hall did as he was asked and stayed by the car until the detective returned, whenever that would be. It actually turned out to be not as long as he'd feared it would be. Bradham returned after only forty-five minutes.

"Done already?" Hall asked. He jokingly turned his phone around to show Bradham the game of solitaire he was playing. "I won."

"Fantastic."

"I thought you'd be a lot longer."

"I got a good look at everything. They're still processing the scene. One of my guys will take the lead on it. I'll get the report."

"Oh."

"Get in my car and we'll go to the station."

"How long's this gonna take? A while?"

"Why, you got plans or something?"

"Well, Charlotte said she was gonna wait for me to get back, so…"

"Better tell her to go to bed, Charlie. You ain't getting any action tonight."

Hall sighed. "I knew it was gonna be a long night."

3

Hall was sitting by a computer in Bradham's office, looking at pictures of various criminals. While he was doing that, he and Bradham continued talking about the case.

"So who was the target here?" Hall asked. "Armstrong or the woman? Or was it both? Was it someone jealous over their affair?"

Bradham extended his cheeks as if he were in pain, but he really was just thinking about the questions. "I dunno, I don't think it's got anything to do with an affair. I don't have anything to base this off of yet, so take it with a grain of salt, but I have a feeling that only one of them was the target. The other was collateral damage."

"What makes you think that?"

"I dunno. Like I said, just a hunch."

"Who was the victim the other time?"

"Woman. Late twenties. Named Carly Learson."

"What was her story?" Hall asked.

"In and out of trouble her whole life. You know the kind."

"Why was she killed?"

"Who knows? Haven't figured out the motive yet. No family. Friends that you could barely classify as that. Nobody seems to know what she was into."

"Work?"

"Whatever she could do to make a dollar."

"Prostitute?"

"Well, I wouldn't call her that. But she would work the streets on occasion if she needed the money. But you could add thief to her name too. She was all over the place on the crime spectrum. Mostly small-time stuff, though. Why someone would wanna kill her is anyone's guess at this point. What about this Armstrong guy? You've been tailing him all week, you said?"

"Yeah."

"See anything suspicious up to now?"

"No, nothing. I've followed him every day for the last six days. He's taken four different women out to dinner, then gone back to their house or apartment for a nightcap, then he goes home."

Bradham got an idea, pulling out a picture of Learson and showing it to Hall. "Was this one of those women?"

Hall looked it over but quickly shook his head. "No, she wasn't one of them."

"Figures."

"Oh, what, you trying to tie the two together?"

"Thought maybe we could start looking at your client. Maybe she hired someone to take out the women involved, and the husband got caught in it too."

"Good thought. I haven't shown her the pictures of the women, though."

"Doesn't mean anything. Maybe she was using you to try to establish an alibi. You know, pretend she doesn't know anything about it, that way she can say she hired you and hadn't seen your report yet. All the while, she already knows, and hired a hitman to take them all out."

"Oh, didn't think of that. That makes sense."

"Possible?"

"I don't think so," Hall replied. "The wife works at a hospital."

"So? I've arrested doctors and nurses before. They're not immune to this stuff."

"Yeah, but if her husband was cheating, she seemed intent on making him pay in a different way."

"You mean financially?"

"Yeah."

"Probably so. This Armstrong didn't meet with anyone else outside of these women?"

"Not while I was tailing him. And I did that after seven o'clock every night."

Bradham leaned back in his chair and rubbed his eyes as he looked up at the ceiling. "I have a feeling this is gonna be one of those cases that keeps me up a lot."

"I thought they all did that."

"This one more than the others."

"So if they were killed the same way, they have a connection to the shooter. Just have to figure out what it is," Hall said.

"Oh, just have to figure out what it is. Just like that."

"Well, I didn't say it was going to be easy."

Bradham pointed to the pictures. "You come up with anything yet?"

"Not yet," Hall answered. "I'm still looking."

"With our luck he won't be in there."

"Who's the woman who got killed tonight?"

Bradham started typing at his computer and looked at the screen. "Wendy Groshens. Thirty-one years old. No major criminal activity, few parking tickets, speeding ticket, yadda yadda."

"Hmm. Thought maybe there'd be a similarity with the other one. Learson. If they were cut from the same cloth, there would be the connection."

"No such luck. They're from completely different sides of the tracks. One had no money, the other was loaded with it."

"What about Armstrong? I don't know much about him other than what his wife told me and the stuff I've seen him do while I was following him."

"Same deal. No major criminal stuff. Parking, speeding tickets, a few of those, nothing else."

"Well, if it's the same shooter, it's not random."

"Ain't gotta tell me," Bradham said. "Just gotta look through the haystack for the needle."

"Watch that it doesn't stick you."

"With my luck it will, and I'll bleed all over the place."

Hall continued looking through mugshots for another twenty minutes before he finally stumbled on one that looked close to the shooter.

"Hey, I think this might be it."

Bradham jumped out of his chair and went over to Hall to look over his shoulder. Hall tapped on the picture.

"Remi Coulson." Bradham then let out a grunt and went back to his desk, sitting down and typing away.

Hall walked over to the detective's desk and sat down as well, wanting more information. "So who's Remi Coulson? Sounds like you know him."

"Know of him. Every police agency in California and probably half the West Coast is looking for him."

"What's he done?"

"Here. Take a look."

Bradham spun his monitor around so Hall could read what they had on the man. Coulson had a lengthy criminal history, punctuated by extreme bouts of violence. He was wanted on murder charges, suspicion of murder, assault, and a dozen other violations in nine states. He now loaned himself out as a gun-for-hire. He didn't come cheap. He was good. When someone hired Coulson, they knew the job was as good as done. And usually his jobs were done mistake-free. He'd wait until the perfect time to strike, and then he was gone. The hit he just did on Armstrong and Groshens was an exception. He hadn't counted on Hall being there. It was actually the closest anyone had ever gotten to Coulson while he was on a job. But he still managed to slip away.

"You should consider yourself lucky," Bradham said.

"How's that?"

"That you're still alive. As you can see, this guy's a bad mamma jamma."

Hall turned the monitor back to its original position when he was done looking at it. Bradham then entered into the computer that Coulson was the chief suspect in the case and put out an APB on him, even though it was probably a waste of time. With Coulson, he was probably already in another county by then. Hall leaned back in his chair and put his hands on top of his head, looking up at the ceiling and thinking about everything. He then sat up straight again after a minute.

"Wait a minute. This doesn't make any sense."

"That's just now coming to you?" Bradham asked.

"What would a professional hitman be doing taking out people like this? Learson, Armstrong, uh,

Groshens... I mean, who would hire him to take out these people?"

"That's the question."

"They're not even dangerous. You could probably hire anybody to do that, right?"

"You're thinking backwards. The first question is why. Why would someone hire him? Once we find out the why, then we might find out the who."

Hall nodded, agreeing with the sentiment. "I'll get started on it in the morning."

"What?"

"I'll start investigating."

"No, no, no. That little license of yours doesn't give you carte blanche to investigate whatever you want. This is an active police investigation. Let us do that."

"Why you gotta be like that? You know I can help."

"It's not about that."

"How many cases have I solved for you so far?"

"A few."

"And this will be another one," Hall said. "I'm working on it whether you like it or not."

"It doesn't even concern you. Why do you wanna get involved?"

"It does concern me. My client's husband was murdered. That's why I wanna get involved. Plus, I'm the guy who tangled with Coulson head-on, nobody else."

"Which you lost, I might add."

"OK, so he got one up on me. But you know what

that all adds up to? I'm already involved. I'm working on it."

Bradham sighed, though he wasn't really as displeased as he sounded. He was actually grateful to get as much help as he could get on the case. Whatever it took to solve it, he was basically all for it. He probably wouldn't have said that for all PIs that he knew, but Hall was an exception. For one, they had become friends, and two, he knew Hall could handle himself if things got rough, unlike some of the people that Bradham knew. He didn't have to worry about Hall walking into a situation that he couldn't handle and then becoming a crime scene himself.

"OK, OK. I'm not gonna give you a hard time about it."

"It's better for your ulcer that you don't," Hall said.

"I don't have an ulcer."

"Not yet."

"But I want you to keep me informed if you find out anything, OK? Or else I will come down hard on you, friend or not."

"You'll be the first to know."

They talked for a few more minutes before Hall decided it was time to go. Bradham didn't need him for anything else.

"Guess I should stop off at Mrs. Armstrong's to talk to her," Hall said.

"I'd wait till the morning if I were you."

"Why?"

"The woman just lost her husband. It's a rough time."

"Yeah, well, she didn't seem that crazy about him lately."

"Just the same," Bradham said. "Based on my experience, she's probably taking it hard, no matter what she thought of him lately or suspected him of. Usually people are given some type of sedative to help them cope, so she might not even be awake now. She'll be more receptive to seeing you in the morning. Just my two cents."

Hall thought about it for a moment. "Yeah, you're probably right. I don't even know if I should tell her about all the stuff he'd been doing this past week. Maybe I should just tell her that he wasn't doing anything. You know, preserve the good memory and all that."

"Brandon, how are you gonna hide the fact her husband was cheating on her? He was found in the bedroom of another woman's home, both of them half-dressed. She knows. You can't hide that from her. The cat's already out of the bag. If she asks, just tell the truth. That's always the best policy. Just tell the truth."

"The truth, right. Yeah. Well, maybe we'll get lucky and she'll actually know something."

"That won't be luck. That'll be a miracle."

4

Hall and Charlotte had just come out of the Armstrong home. Hall wanted his girlfriend to come along, figuring she could relate to Mrs. Armstrong better than he could in that situation. Plus, she might have felt better talking to another woman in a time like that. Bradham was right. Truth was the best policy, and Hall laid it all out there for her. Though it was obviously hard to hear about her husband's infidelities, she was grateful for knowing the truth. It still hurt that he was killed, but maybe it would provide some relief for her, knowing that she was going to divorce him anyway. It was tough to say, but Hall thought she'd pull through it OK.

"I can't believe you brought me here for that," Charlotte said, getting in their car.

"What? You always say you want to help and get involved."

"You were just afraid of talking to her yourself and telling her that her husband was cheating."

"I was not afraid."

"Yes, you were. Don't deny it."

"I just figured she might need a shoulder to cry on, and she might be more willing to do that with you than with me. Plus, women are more relaxed around other women, and she might talk more if you were there."

"You think so, huh?"

"Isn't that true?"

"Don't quit this job. A psychiatrist you're not." Hall shrugged and started driving away from the house. "Where are we going now?"

"Well, I guess I'll drop you off at the apartment and then I'll—"

"No, no, no, stop right there. You are not going to do that."

"What?"

"You're not going to use me for the dirty jobs, then get rid of me when you wanna do something else."

"I'm not."

"Yes, you are," Charlotte said. "You use me for the crying woman, then when you wanna investigate, oh, let's drop her off and get rid of her. It doesn't work like that, pal."

"Pal?"

"Yeah, pal! I'm either in this or I'm not."

"That's not what I'm doing."

"Well, I'm just telling you."

"I thought you had design work to do and was—"

"No, you wanted to dump me. Just admit it."

"I would never dump you."

"I'm just saying. I don't have design work to do. Well, I do, but I can do it later. You know, that's the benefit of working from home. It can suit your schedule."

"Someone's a little testy today."

"Well, you're not gonna treat me like some, some... I don't know what. But you're not gonna do it."

"Charlotte, relax. You might bust or something."

"I just want to let you know that we're partners. Partners do things together. You're not gonna shy away from me 'cause you don't want me to get hurt or any of that other nonsense you're thinking."

Hall thought about continuing the argument, then thought better of it. She was already worked up, and the more he thought about it, he couldn't really dispute anything she was saying. She wasn't wrong. He just wanted her to be safe, but he knew that he couldn't control what she did. She was his partner. He hoped for the rest of his life.

"OK, you win."

"So you're not gonna fight me about going with you now?" Charlotte asked.

"No, I'm not gonna fight you. Whatever you want to do."

Charlotte clapped her hands happily. "So where are we going?"

"I don't know."

"What?"

"I'm not sure where we're going."

"You mean after all that, you don't have a plan in mind?"

"Not particularly," he said.

"I should've saved my rant for a better time!"

Hall smiled, and the next time they stopped at a light, he leaned over and kissed her.

"I've got it!" Hall said.

"You've got what?"

"I know what to do."

"You should kiss me more often. See all the good things that happen when you do? Inspiration strikes you."

Hall laughed. "Oh, is that what it is?"

"Yep."

"Well, I don't know about that. I can agree about doing it more often, though."

As they started driving again, Hall took a turn, and Charlotte could tell that they weren't going back to the apartment anymore.

"You wanna tell me where we're going?"

"Back to the apartment to work."

"This is not the way to the apartment."

"I figured we could stop and pick up lunch first," Hall said. "We might be awhile."

"Oh. OK. What exactly are we going to be working on?"

"We're gonna figure out what these women were into."

"Women? So you're assuming Armstrong was innocent?"

"Yes."

"Why?"

"Just a feeling. I think the women were the targets and there's a connection there. I think Armstrong was in the wrong place at the wrong time."

"That's a big hunch."

"Well, considering they were killed in Groshens' home, that would indicate she was the target, right? I mean, I doubt you would follow Armstrong there and kill him along with someone else. If he was alone all day while his wife was at work, you could've just killed him there without worrying about the second body."

"That makes sense."

"So I have a feeling there's a connection between Groshens and Learson. I know they were on different sides of the tracks, like Bradham said, but there's a connection. There has to be."

"Won't the police be looking for the same connection?"

"Yeah. But we'll do it better."

"How you figure?"

Hall smiled. "'Cause I have you."

After going through a fast-food drive-through, Hall and Charlotte went back to their apartment to start working. Charlotte took the lead since she was the computer expert. She dug into the backgrounds of all three victims, printing out everything about them. They looked at their criminal histories, job histories, addresses, relatives, schools, everything that could be traced to them. The two of them then started combing through it all.

"You know, the police are going to be looking at the same exact stuff," Charlotte said.

"I know. But it's like the old adage says, two people can look at the same picture and come up with two different conclusions. Or something like that. Just because you're looking at the same information doesn't mean you'll come up with the same response."

"True. So what are we looking for again?"

"Anything that might seem weird, out of place, or anything that might connect all of them together. Or two of them together."

"I don't see any connection here at all," Charlotte said. "I mean, the guy worked at a bank, Learson was… whatever she was, and Groshens was an insurance executive."

"Maybe they had a similar group of friends."

"From what you said, Learson didn't have friends."

"According to Bradham, she was distant from everybody."

"Well, somebody knew her well enough to kill her," Charlotte replied.

"There's a connection. This guy, Coulson, isn't just

picking names out of a hat. There's a connection somewhere. Somewhere."

They continued looking through all the information they had, and Charlotte even went back on the computer to dig through more records, hoping they could find that needle in the haystack. After several hours of an exhaustive search, they came to the same conclusion as when they'd started. They had nothing.

"This is impossible," Charlotte said, running her fingers through her hair. "There is nothing here. Nothing."

"Nothing's impossible."

"Brandon, we have been looking at this stuff for three hours now. And we are no closer to finding anything than when we started."

"Can't give up."

"I'm not saying to give up. But I think we might need to rethink our strategy here."

"To what?" Hall said, still looking through the papers.

"That maybe there really isn't a connection. These people may not know each other at all."

"At least two of them know the same person. I believe that."

"Well, if they do, we're not finding it in here."

"Maybe not. But it's there. Guess we'll have to hit the pavement."

"And do what?"

"Start knocking on doors," Hall answered.

"Which door are you knocking on first?"

"Learson."

Charlotte rolled her eyes and groaned. "Why her?"

"Because she lived in the building that would probably give us the best information."

"I thought she lived in some dump of an apartment complex."

"She did. That's why that's the best one. It'll be easier to find someone willing to talk."

"Didn't the police already do that?"

"Yeah, but they're not able to bribe people."

"And we are?"

"We are."

"We don't have that much money, Brandon."

"Just a little bit. Twenty, fifty, shouldn't take much more than that."

"Good, 'cause we don't have much more than that!"

"We'll be fine."

"We have to go to another one of those dirty apartment complexes? Really?"

Hall laughed. "I know how much you love it so."

"I do not."

"Yeah, but this is part of the job, right? I mean, if you wanna be my partner, and you wanna help out, sometimes you gotta go to the dirty, dingy, smelly places to get what you want."

Charlotte sighed, already starting to mentally prepare herself. "Should I bring along my frying pan?"

Hall snickered. "If you can fit it in your purse."

5

Before driving over to Learson's apartment, Hall first stopped at an ATM and took out fifty dollars in case they needed to use it for incentives. As he drove away, he could feel Charlotte staring at him. He turned and looked, and sure enough, she was burning a hole right through him.

"What?"

"I can't believe we're actually taking money out of our own bank account for this."

Hall shrugged. "This is what it takes sometimes."

"Our own personal money. And we're not even getting paid for this, you know. Even if we solve this case, we get nothing out of it."

"We get the experience and satisfaction of knowing we solved it and got a bad guy off the streets."

"That's all well and good, but it doesn't exactly help pay the bills."

"The more experience we have, the more cases we solve, the more we can brag about the things we've done, which should bring us more business, right?"

Charlotte didn't want to admit that he might have been right, so she begrudgingly agreed. "I guess so. In theory, at least."

"It's not like we're throwing away a few hundred dollars or something. We can afford this."

"For now."

"Relax. It'll be fine."

Once they finally arrived at the apartment complex, Hall found an empty spot, which wasn't too hard, considering it looked like only half the spaces had been filled. Before getting out of the car, Charlotte sat there, staring at the building.

"This has got to be the worst one yet."

Hall smiled. "I dunno. Looks like it has a little charm to it."

"Charm? You call that charm?"

"Maybe for someone."

"Brandon, there are shingles missing on the roof, a couple of windows that look like someone got thrown through them, siding that was torn off, or that they took off when they couldn't wash the blood off of it, a couple of shady looking characters sitting by the side there, and a couple boards by whatever used to be there. It literally looks like a dump."

"So it needs some work," Hall said, taking some

pleasure in how anxious she got over visiting places like this. He enjoyed egging her on for some reason.

"Work? Uh, there is not enough work available to fix this place. This thing needs to be torn down."

"Maybe they're letting it happen naturally."

"Better happen soon. Looks like a good thunderstorm might do the trick and knock it over."

Hall smiled and let her rant for another couple of minutes. "You done now?"

"Yeah, I guess so."

"You coming in or staying here?"

Charlotte glared at him. "Are you kidding? You really think I'm gonna stay here by myself?"

"Just thought I'd ask."

"What do I always tell you? The safest place for me to be is right behind you."

"Even in places like this?"

"Especially places like this," Charlotte replied. "It's better to be behind you and possibly get into trouble than not be near you at all and definitely get into trouble."

"I think you're a bit dramatic."

"Yeah, well, maybe. But the thought is still the same."

"Can we go in now?"

Charlotte took a deep breath. "If we have to."

They went inside the building, passing a few rough-looking characters. Charlotte looked straight ahead the entire time. Hall smiled and shook his head at her, amused by her fear. They went up via the stairs to Learson's second-floor apartment. Once they found her room, they saw police tape across the door. Hall took a quick look around, then started picking at the lock.

"What are you doing?" Charlotte asked, looking around to see if anyone was watching.

"What's it look like I'm doing?"

"It looks like you're breaking in."

"See? Who said you didn't know what was going on?"

"Brandon, you can't do that."

"Why not?"

"It's illegal."

"There's no one here."

"It's still illegal," Charlotte said, pointing at the yellow tape. "See what that says? Do not cross. You're crossing!"

"Who's gonna tell?"

Hall got the door open and ducked under the caution tape. Charlotte took one more look around, then rushed in with her boyfriend. She certainly wasn't going to stand out there by herself, illegal or not. She was going where he was. They closed the door behind them, then started looking around.

"What are we looking for?"

"Beats me," Hall answered. "Anything that looks interesting."

"The police have already done this. I'm sure they

took anything that looks interesting."

"Probably. Doesn't hurt to check and see if they missed anything, though."

They spent the next half hour going through the one-bedroom apartment, not that there was a lot to see. There wasn't much in the way of furnishings. There were the basics and nothing more. It was a little messy with some clothes and trash on the floor, but they didn't find anything that would provide them with a clue as to what Learson was mixed up in.

After coming out of the apartment, they saw the door across the hall was open. Hall went over to it and knocked. The resident quickly came over and answered. She was middle-aged, probably in her late forties. She had short, balding hair, missing teeth, and scars on her arms. It looked like she had done some serious living in her time.

"Excuse me, did you know the woman across the hall?" Hall asked.

"Who you?"

"Uh, I'm an investigator. My name's Brandon Hall. We're investigating her death."

"Cops were here the otha day."

"Yes, I know, and we're following up on their initial findings. Did you talk to them?"

"For a spell."

"Anything you can add to that?"

"Nah. Didn't see nuthin, didn't hear nuthin, don't know nuthin."

"Oh." Hall smiled. "Makes it pretty simple then, doesn't it?"

"Sure as does."

"OK. Well, thanks for your time."

"Yap."

The woman closed the door. Hall and Charlotte stood there for a second, looking at each other.

"Well, that was interesting," Hall said.

"I hope she wasn't the best of the bunch that we'll talk to."

Hall made a face, suggesting that he wasn't sure that wouldn't be the case. They went to one of Learson's neighbors who lived directly next to her. A man answered the door. After chatting for a few minutes, they determined that he didn't know anything either. His appearance and demeanor was only mildly better than the last person they'd talked to. They tried another door. This time they didn't even get an answer.

"Maybe they're out," Charlotte said.

"I can hear a TV."

"Maybe they're hard of hearing."

"Or they just don't wanna talk."

"Some people don't answer the door if they don't know who it is."

"Yeah, I know. On to the next one," Hall said.

They moved down the line to another door. This time, a teenager answered. He actually looked like a normal kid, and he was about seventeen, maybe eighteen years old.

"Help you?"

"Hi. My name's Brandon. We're investigating the death of Ms. Learson over there. I was wondering if you could help us."

A woman started shouting from inside the apartment. "Wait, wait, wait, we're not talking about anything to do with that." A woman in her mid-thirties appeared. She was thin, long black hair that went down past her shoulders, and she had an attractive face.

"My son's not talking to anyone about that."

"Did you talk to the police the other day?" Hall asked.

"I did. We don't know anything. I already told the police that. We didn't know the lady, didn't talk to her, never saw anything."

"What about your son?"

"He doesn't know anything either," she said.

"Mind if we talk to him?"

"I said he doesn't know anything."

"Did the police talk to him the other day?"

"No, he was out."

Hall kept glancing at the young man, getting the feeling from his body language that what he was hearing wasn't exactly the truth. Every time his mother spoke, the kid looked down at the ground. That was a sign to Hall that maybe there was more to the story than what they were telling.

"Mrs...." Hall said, trying to lead her into telling him her name.

"It's Ms. I'm not married anymore. Berkely."

"Ms. Berkely. It would really be a big help if you could help us with this. Anything you know could go a long way to helping us figure out who did this."

"That girl, Carly, she was no good. There were men coming in and out of that place constantly. Loud noises, drugs, parties, I'm not sorry she's gone."

"Ms. Berkely, I'm not here to say whether anyone was a good person or not. I didn't know her. But I am here to say that no one deserves to be murdered."

"I've got an ex-husband that I would disagree with you on."

Hall smiled. "Be that as it may... the person who killed Carly also killed two other people. One was a banker, the other was an insurance executive. Now, the man that did this has now killed three people. I don't think they deserved it either, do you?"

Ms. Berkely looked down. "I'm sorry about that. But that don't change nothing here."

"And your son? I get the feeling that he may know more than you give him credit for."

"Why are you looking into all this? You don't sound like you're with the police."

"We're not. We're private investigators. One of our clients, her husband, was one of the victims. We want to find the man who killed him."

Ms. Berkely looked down at the ground again and

started shaking her head. Hall thought he might have been getting through to her, but she needed a little extra push.

"Ms. Berkely, anything that you tell us will be kept right here. Nobody else needs to know."

"What about the police?"

Hall briefly looked at Charlotte. "As far as I'm concerned, they don't need to know unless you want them to."

"I don't."

"Well then, I don't see why anyone other than the three of us needs to know."

"And if you talk to the police about it, and they ask you where you got the information?"

"I can't remember where I got it. Somebody gave me an anonymous phone call. Somebody slipped me a piece of paper. Somebody sent me an email." Hall shrugged. "We can go on and on."

"You're sure? Because if this comes back to us, I'll deny everything."

"I give you my word. Whatever you tell us will be confidential."

"Well, I guess you guys should come in then so we're not standing out here in the hallway where all the rest of these degenerates can see and hear us."

Hall and Charlotte went inside so they could talk in private. It looked to them like they had found the needle that they were looking for.

6

Ms. Berkely offered Hall and Charlotte a drink, which they accepted, thinking it would help to put everyone at ease. They were all for anything that would make everyone talk more freely. Ms. Berkely and her son came out of the kitchen with four glasses of iced tea for everyone. Hall took a sip as his hosts sat down on the couch across from them.

"Wow, that's delicious."

Charlotte took a sip as well. "Yeah, that's really good."

Ms. Berkely smiled. "It's homemade."

"Fantastic," Hall said. He then cleared his throat, trying to ease into his questions as naturally as possible, even though they all knew that's what he was there for. "So what do you know about Carly?"

"First of all, we don't know anything about the night she was killed. We didn't see anything."

"OK. What about before that?"

Ms. Berkely turned to her son. "This is my son, Nick. About two days before she was killed, he came out of our apartment and noticed Carly arguing with some guy near the steps that lead downstairs."

"Did you hear what they were talking about?"

Nick coughed and looked at his mother, who nodded at him. "Uh, yeah, I heard a little."

"What were they saying?"

"The man was saying how she wasn't sticking to the plan, and she was talking too much to people about it. Then she was saying that she needed more money to keep doing the job."

"What job?"

"I don't know. They never really said what it was."

"Did they say anything else?"

"The man grabbed her arm real tight a couple of times. At first I thought he was gonna rough her up some, but he didn't. I kind of just stayed by the door for a few minutes. I was kind of afraid to go near them at first, so I just waited until they were done."

"They never saw you?"

"No, I stayed real still."

"What else did they say?"

"Something about how the scam was working really good so far. At least that's what the guy was saying. He said they didn't need to be changing anything, and how she needed to lock things down on her end."

"And what'd she say?"

"She just kept saying that she would do what she wanted, and how she wanted a bigger cut of things. Eventually the guy got mad and just kind of left."

"You ever see this guy before?"

"Yeah, I think I saw him come out of the building once, maybe last month, something like that. I was playing basketball outside and saw him. He didn't look like someone I had seen around before, that's why I remembered him."

"Do you think you could identify him from a picture?" Charlotte asked.

"I think so."

"Wait a minute," Ms. Berkely said. "We're not going anywhere for him to identify anybody."

"No, no," Hall said. "We didn't mean anything like that. What I said before still stands. If we were somehow able to get some pictures of people similar to the guy your son described, would you be able to pick him out?"

"I can draw you a picture of him if you want," Nick said.

"You can?"

Ms. Berkely smiled. "My son is an excellent artist. It's what he eventually wants to go to school for. Something that he can use his talents on."

Nick got up and went over to the desk in the corner of the room. He took out his drawing notebook from a drawer and started sketching the man. As he was doing that, Hall and Charlotte continued talking to his mother.

"He's a good kid," Ms. Berkely said. "He deserves better than being here."

"If you don't mind me asking," Hall said, "why are you here?"

"Hopefully it's not for too much longer. His father left us about… oh, about five years ago now. It's been a constant struggle since then. It's been hard. Paying the bills, putting food on the table, a roof over our heads. It hasn't been easy with just me working. We had a house, but I couldn't afford that anymore. Then it's been one apartment after another these past few years, each time downgrading to a cheaper one. That's how we ended up here. We've been here close to a year. I can't wait to move. I've been trying to save up some extra money, work a couple extra shifts, overtime when it's available, all so we can go to a nicer place."

Hall reached into his pocket and removed the fifty dollars they'd withdrawn from the bank earlier. He tried to hand it to Ms. Berkely, who put her hand up, refusing to take it.

"No, no, thank you. We'll be fine."

"I want you guys to have it," Hall said.

"We don't take charity here. We work for everything we have and want."

"It's not charity. We intended to give this to whoever was able to provide us with good information. Consider it a bonus."

Ms. Berkely smiled. "Thank you. I appreciate the thought, but it wouldn't seem right."

"Does Nick have any colleges picked out yet?" Charlotte asked.

"He's got his eye on a couple. He's not planning on leaving home, though. I gave him my blessing if he wanted to explore the world, live on campus somewhere, but he doesn't wanna leave me. He's a good kid. He even picked up a part-time job a couple months ago to try to help with everything."

"That's nice."

"Yeah, but I don't want him working too much. I want him to concentrate on his grades, maybe get some kind of scholarship somewhere to help with costs, even if it's only a partial one."

"With you in his corner, I'm sure he'll be fine," Hall said.

A few minutes later, Nick came back over to the group with a detailed drawing of the man he saw. He handed it to Hall, who looked it over.

"This is amazing detail," Hall said, showing it to his girlfriend.

"Wow, you are really talented," Charlotte gushed. "This is as good as anything. Very detailed."

Nick smiled, glad they liked his work. As Charlotte was looking at the picture, Hall got up and walked over to the desk, seeing Nick's workbook on the desk.

"Mind if I look through it?" Hall asked, genuinely interested in the kid's work.

Dark Day

"Yeah, go ahead."

Hall looked through the drawings and sketches, a few of which hadn't been finished yet. But there was no denying the talent. And the kid had that in spades.

"This is great, work, man. It really is. I hope you stick with it. You got a gift with this."

"I will," Nick replied.

The group chatted for a few more minutes, asking a few more questions about the man that Nick had drawn. The Berkelys didn't know anything other than what they had already said, though. But still, it was a start for Hall and Charlotte. They had a leg up on the police now, who didn't have this information yet. Hall and Charlotte finally left. Nick escorted them to the door. Once they were outside, Hall again tried to pass the money off.

"Here," Hall said, holding the money out.

"Oh, nah, my mom wouldn't want me to take it."

"Why are you guys so stubborn with this?" Hall asked with a laugh. "You did good, and you might help solve this murder by helping out. You should take it."

Nick shook his head. "My mom always says you should try to do the right thing without looking for a reward. I think she felt bad that she was trying to hide all this at first. She knew it wasn't right."

"So why did she?" Charlotte asked. "I mean, not tell the police."

"She didn't want me to get mixed up in it. You always hear stories about witnesses and trials and people getting even and stuff like that. She didn't want any of that to happen to me."

Hall nodded, understanding the reasoning. He didn't blame them. But he still wanted them to have the money. He fully expected to pay someone before they left for the day anyway, at least if he gave it to them, he figured it would be going to a good place. At least they wouldn't waste it on drugs, booze, or prostitutes, like he pictured someone else doing. Well, presumably none of those things, anyway. It was always possible he misevaluated them. But he didn't think so.

"Here," Hall said, taking Nick's hand and putting the money in it. "Tell your mom you got a bonus from work or something."

Nick smiled. "I don't know if she'll believe that. I try not to lie to her."

"You're a good kid. Take her out to dinner or something. She deserves it."

"She does. And probably a lot more than that."

Hall tapped the kid on the shoulder before he and Charlotte left. "Take it easy, huh?"

"I will."

"And don't worry, we'll never say where we got it."

"Good luck."

Hall and Charlotte left the building and went back to their car. It couldn't have been quick enough for Charlotte. Though they actually weren't in there for as long as she had expected, the sooner they left the better, as far as she was concerned. Before driving off, they talked about what they'd learned.

"So what do we do now?" Charlotte asked.

Hall held up the picture of the man that Nick drew. "We find out who this guy is."

"How are we gonna do that?"

"Take it down to Bradham and see."

"He's not gonna like that."

Hall smiled. "I know."

7

Hall and Charlotte went down to the police station to see Bradham, though they had a little bit of a wait. The detective was already in a conference with some other members of the department, so they wound up sitting for about half an hour.

"I'll bet when he sees us, he throws his hands up in frustration," Hall said.

"Don't be smart."

"Or maybe he'll turn and go in the other direction."

"Or maybe he'll just be glad to see us," Charlotte said.

Hall snickered. "Yeah, I'm pretty sure that's one reaction we won't get."

"Why do you always do that to him?"

"Because he hates it when we upstage him."

"It's not a competition, Brandon."

"I know. I'm not competing. He just thinks it should

always be them who investigates and solves everything."

"I think he'll be fine."

"You really don't know him, do you?" Hall asked.

Once the half hour was up, Bradham started walking down the hall, visible to his guests. He didn't look up at all, though. He had his head buried in a file folder as he walked. Hall and Charlotte started to walk over to him so they could catch him before he got to his office. Bradham finally peered up from his folder and caught a glimpse of the two people walking toward him.

"Oh, no!" Bradham then turned around for a second before turning back again to face them.

Hall laughed and nudged Charlotte in the arm. "See, told you." Charlotte made a face, not happy that he was right again. "Is that really a nice way to greet us?"

"What do you want?"

"What did I do?" Charlotte innocently asked.

"No, not you," Bradham said, giving his friend a brief hug. "Sorry, you're fine."

"Hey, what did I do?" Hall asked.

"'Cause you're a pain in my ass."

"All I did was…"

"Yeah, yeah, yeah, what do you want? What are you here for?"

Hall looked at Charlotte and shook his head. "See?

We're here to help him, and this is the thanks we get. A grumpy, overworked, irritated, not nice..."

"Yeah, yeah, we get the point. Now what do you want?"

"Oh, we're just here with new information on the case. You said to keep you updated."

"What do you have?"

Hall pointed to Charlotte's purse, where she was keeping the picture that Nick drew. She took it out and handed it to the detective.

"What's this?" Bradham asked.

"You mean who's this," Hall said.

"Yeah, whatever, what's it about?"

"This guy was seen having a heated argument with Learson. What was it, a week or two before she was killed?"

"Yeah, about that," Charlotte replied.

"How do you know this?" Bradham asked.

"We got it from a source."

"What source? We talked to everyone in that building. Nobody admitted to seeing or knowing anything."

Hall had a smug look on his face. "Guess you didn't talk to the right people."

"Or had fifty dollars in your hand," Charlotte said.

Bradham looked at her for a second, then at Hall. "Fifty dollars? You mean to tell me you're paying for information? Bribing people?"

"We didn't bribe anyone," Hall answered. "I was going to offer it, but they wound up telling me anyway.

Dark Day

So it wasn't necessary. Maybe you need to change your tactics."

"If the police department started paying people for tips, we'd go broke."

Bradham then kept walking and headed for his office. Hall and Charlotte followed him in, closing the door for privacy. Bradham sat behind his desk and looked at the picture.

"So where'd you get this?"

"Can't tell you," Hall replied.

Bradham took his eyes off the drawing and gave his friend a stern look. "Really?"

"I told them I wouldn't say where it came from."

"Brandon, if we wind up catching this guy, we'll need them to testify in court about what they saw."

Hall shook his head. "Won't happen. They won't testify. They don't wanna be involved."

"Well, they are involved. If they saw this man arguing with Learson, that gives him a motive. If we find this guy, and then find other evidence supporting that, then, with an eyewitness, we can tie him and Learson together. If not, we may not have a way of proving they were together. We'll need them to talk."

"Like I said, won't happen. I told them I wouldn't say where it came from, and I won't."

"If push came to shove, you could be ordered to provide that information, you know."

Hall shook his head. "No. I won't. I mean, if it meant me going to jail, then so be it. I wouldn't say where it came from. I gave them my word and I meant it. We'll find another way."

Bradham looked at Charlotte. "How do you put up with him?"

"It's not easy sometimes."

Hall looked at Charlotte and raised his eyebrows. "Really?"

Charlotte just flashed one of her innocent looking smiles at him.

Bradham sighed and looked at the drawing again. "OK, OK, we'll say it came from an anonymous source for right now, OK?"

Hall gave a slight nod. "OK. I mean, I said I would give you new information that I had, and I am, so if you're gonna give me problems, I'll just take my business elsewhere."

"Elsewhere? Like who?"

Hall thought for a few seconds. "I dunno. Isn't there a new lieutenant that just got promoted? I'm sure he'd appreciate cracking a big case after just getting bumped up a notch. Make him look really good."

Bradham's eyes bulged out. "You'd really give your information to some guy you don't even know over me?"

"Well, you seem to give me a hard time every time I talk to you, so…"

"All right, all right, let's just drop the whole thing."

"Now, should we look through the books and see if we can find out who this guy is?"

Bradham continued looking at the drawing. "This is really good. Who did it?"

Hall waved his finger at him. "Nuh-uh. You're not gonna find out that way."

Bradham rolled his eyes.

"Let's just say it wasn't an adult, would that satisfy you?" Charlotte said.

Hall turned and looked at her, peeved that she even let that much information slip. He flipped over his hands as if he were angry that she'd even spoken.

"What? It still doesn't tell him anything?"

"Now he can check out every resident in that building and see who's got kids under eighteen and narrow it down," Hall replied.

"Oh. I didn't think of that."

Bradham laughed. "Yeah. I could do that. I won't. But I could. For now, I'll respect the agreement you had with whoever this was."

"Like I said, it wouldn't do you any good. If this was a person under eighteen, their guardians would never let them get involved anyway, so you'd just be wasting your time."

"A kid did this, huh? This is good work. Almost as good as our sketch artists."

"I know, isn't it?"

"All right, let's pull the computers up and see if we can figure out who this mug is," Bradham said. He pulled out his laptop, turned it on and logged in, then he slid it across the table. "Here. You guys look through here while I go through it on this one. You start at the beginning, I'll start at the end. We can knock it out faster if we do it together."

"Works for me," Hall replied.

The three of them started looking through the photos of criminals, hoping they'd get lucky. The assumption was that the man they were looking for was in there somewhere. Unless the guy was just lucky enough to never have been caught, which seemed unlikely, or he was too young to get locked up yet. That didn't seem to be the case either, since the guy they were looking for appeared to be in his late thirties or early forties. It was doubtful this was his first rodeo in terms of breaking the law.

An hour went by, neither party having much luck. Hall went to the cafeteria to get them some coffee. Only a few minutes after returning, it seemed their luck had changed.

"Wait," Bradham said. "I think I got him." He looked at the drawing again, then back to his computer, doing this a couple of times to make sure he had the right man. And he was. "This is him."

"Who?" Hall said, leaning over the desk to see.

"Go to the T's. Walter Thurmond."

Charlotte immediately went to that name. "That's him."

"Almost the spitting image," Hall said. "Drawing is dead on."

"It is," Bradham said.

They began reading Thurmond's information. And it was a lot to go over. He'd been in local jail, county jail, and federal prison in the past twenty years. He was forty-three years old and seemed like a career criminal, constantly in and out of jail since becoming an adult.

"This guy's been in jail five times since he turned eighteen," Hall said.

"That's what we call a lifer," Bradham replied.

"Well, that would fit with Learson all right. Now we just gotta find him."

"Even if we do, doesn't mean he killed her."

"That's right," Charlotte said. "There's nothing in here that says he's a violent guy. Of all his crimes, there's no assaults, murders, rapes, nothing violent."

Bradham nodded. "Of course, it also doesn't mean he didn't finally make the jump."

"Yeah, but you said these look like professional hits," Hall said. "Does this guy really seem the type to put one in the chest and one in the head his first time killing people? It'd probably be a little sloppier, wouldn't it?"

"Yeah, probably. You never know with some of these people, though."

"Or it could mean we have something bigger on our hands. Something a lot more involved with a lot more players."

Bradham sighed, not liking the possibility, even though he knew it might have been more likely. "Yeah. I'm gonna put into the system that he's wanted for questioning. So if someone spots him, they'll pick him up. I'll also talk to some of his known associates."

Charlotte's eyes widened upon seeing the list of names that Thurmond was associated with. "There's no shortage of them, are there? Jeez, there must be fifty names on this list."

Bradham smiled. "Yeah, well, when you've been at it as long as Thurmond has, you're bound to expand your Rolodex at some point."

"Can we print this out?" Hall asked. "We'll start running down some of the names too."

Bradham nodded. "Go ahead."

"What? No argument this time?"

"With as many names that are listed here, I'll take all the help I can get. Even if it's from you."

"You're so thoughtful."

"Print out a second copy of that list."

Charlotte hit the print button again, so Bradham went over to the printer and grabbed the two copies. He then grabbed a pen and circled the top half of the list on one of the printouts and the bottom half on the other one. He handed one to Hall.

"Here, no sense duplicating our efforts and questioning the same people. You take half and we'll take half."

"Well, there's only two of us and you got probably a dozen people at your disposal," Hall said. "You'll probably get through it a lot faster than we will."

"Hey, you wanted in, you got in. Are you complaining?"

Hall briefly looked at Charlotte. "Uh, no. No complaint."

"Great. I guess you better get cracking then, huh?"

"How 'bout the addresses that are listed here for these people?"

"What about them?"

"Are they still good, you think?"

Bradham shrugged. "Eh. Some might be, some I can guarantee almost definitely will not be."

"Great."

"Oh, don't look so glum. I mean, you're a private detective now, right? You should be able to run these people down in no time."

Hall faked a smile, obviously not amused at Bradham's attempt at humor. He and Charlotte then left the building and walked to their car. Charlotte got into the driver's seat.

"Where to?"

Hall looked at the paper and sighed. "Guess we might as well start at the top of the list."

"Gonna be a long day."

Hall nodded. "It certainly will."

8
―――

Hall and Charlotte spent the rest of the day trying to run down the known associates of Walter Thurmond. They actually found a handful of them, right at the addresses they were supposed to be at. But none of them admitted to talking to Thurmond recently. Not one of them said they had even seen Thurmond in the last few months. It was somewhat disappointing, but they knew it was part of the process of running down leads.

By the time the day was over, Hall and Charlotte wound up talking to eight people. That wasn't bad, but they still had a very healthy amount to go. Once they got back to their apartment, they both plopped themselves down on the couch to try to relax.

"Did you ever finish that job you were working on?" Hall asked.

Charlotte thought for a minute, not initially

Dark Day

remembering what he was talking about. "Oh, no, but that's not due for a few more days. I still have time."

"Oh. I just didn't want you to miss your deadline."

"Even if it was tonight, I don't think I could do it," Charlotte said, stretching her legs out. "I'm so beat."

"Just think, we get to do it all over again tomorrow."

Charlotte tilted her head and stared at him. "Really?"

Hall shrugged. "Just saying."

"I'm not looking forward to it. You hungry?"

Hall put his hand on his stomach. "Not really. I'm still full from what we grabbed earlier. You?"

"Not really. Just wondered if you were."

"Oh. No."

They put the TV on, though neither really had anything particular in mind that they wanted to watch. It turned out that they didn't watch much of anything, anyway. In a matter of minutes, they had both fallen asleep, eventually sleeping on top of one another during the night. Hall was the first one awake the following morning, though not by much. When he started squirming to wake up, his movements nudged Charlotte to do the same.

This time, after washing himself off, Hall went into the kitchen and made breakfast. By the time Charlotte got out of the shower, food was already on the table.

"Well, this is a nice change," Charlotte said, sitting down to eat her eggs.

"Hey, it's not gourmet or anything, but at least it's edible."

Charlotte leaned over and gave her boyfriend a kiss. "Thank you. It's very nice."

"I figured you usually make everything, so I thought I'd give you a break for once."

"I appreciate that."

After they were done eating, they grabbed their list of names and started making plans. In order to work on their list more efficiently, they mapped out the addresses, trying to group together those that were nearest each other, that way the commute times would be shorter. Once they were ready, they went down to their car and started driving.

"I wonder how Bradham's making out so far," Charlotte said.

"Probably no better than we are."

"Maybe you should check to see if he came up with anything."

"I think he would've told us if he did," Hall said.

"Maybe you should check anyway, just in case. That way we're not driving around for nothing."

"Yeah, I guess."

Hall pulled out his phone and dialed Bradham's number. He didn't immediately pick up, and instead it went to voicemail. Hall left a message, telling him what they were up to for the day. Bradham returned the call less than five minutes later.

"Hey, just got your message," Bradham said.

"How you making out?"

"By what you said in the message, same as you are."

"Eh, was hoping you were doing better than us."

"Nah, no such luck. Talked to about ten people yesterday. One of which actually admitted to seeing Thurmond a few weeks ago."

"Oh? Any details?"

"Just said he saw him at a local bar or something. Said hi to him, nothing more than that really."

"Maybe we should check the bar out."

"Save your gas, I've already done that," Bradham said. "It's nothing. Nobody there remembers seeing Thurmond in the place. He's not a regular it seems, and nobody that works there knows his face from the picture we showed them."

"Maybe the guy's not being truthful about the extent of their meeting."

"Eh, I don't know. We questioned him pretty thoroughly. He never slipped up on his story at all. I got the feeling he was telling the truth. I don't think he knows anything more than that."

"That's too bad. Well, we're on our way to our first name for the day."

"Keep pushing. We'll eventually find someone who knows him. That's the thing about these guys. Once they know someone, they tend to stick with them and do business over and over again. Somebody should know something."

"Just hope it doesn't take too long to find them," Hall said.

"Just keep grinding. Like I said, something will break."

If something was going to break like Bradham said, it sure didn't look like it would with the help of Hall and Charlotte. At least that's how they viewed it. They spent half the day talking to a few more people on their list, still coming up with nothing. They were starting to get discouraged, thinking they were wasting their time. But it still had to be done. They knew that. They just wished they'd get something, anything, the tiniest of little nuggets that they could act on. It didn't seem to be coming, though. They eventually got through the day, checking off another nine names on the list. It was the same as the previous day. No leads to check. They went home again, doing the same as the night before, falling asleep on the couch together.

They woke up early the next day, ready to get to work again, hoping that they would finally find what we're looking for. Before getting started, they called Bradham again to check his progress. It was the same as the day before. Nothing new or interesting to report. They mapped out their itinerary, just as they had the previous day.

"Ready to go?" Charlotte asked.

Hall nodded. "We got eight more names left. Hopefully one of these can give us something."

"I wouldn't hold your breath."

"I'm not."

They proceeded to talk to four more people on their list. None of them had anything of interest to tell them. Nobody knew anything, nobody saw anything, and nobody heard anything.

"Let's just go back to the apartment and figure out our next move," Charlotte said. "This is all a waste of time. We're not finding anything, and we're not gonna find anything."

Hall didn't necessarily disagree with the sentiment, but they only had a few more names to go. Might as well finish it off. "We got four names left. Let's just talk to them so we don't leave anything left to chance. Who knows? Maybe one of these will be the jackpot."

"Smoking pot is more like it you mean."

They talked to two more people with the same result. The next person on the list was a man named Melvin Hyde. As they drove over to the address they had for him, Hall looked over some of his information.

"This address sounds familiar."

"I swear if it's another dump, I'm gonna..." Charlotte said, not finishing her sentence.

"You're gonna what?"

"I don't know. I really hope it's a somewhat decent looking place for a change."

"You know what the odds of that are?"

"About the same as this guy actually knowing anything?"

"Probably."

Once they got to Hyde's address, they were actually somewhat surprised. Nobody would say they were in what would be described as the nice part of town, as there were more than a few buildings in need of repairs, but Hyde's place wasn't too bad. It was certainly better than what they pictured before they got there. It wouldn't be described as anybody's dream home, but it wasn't falling apart, and it looked clean from the outside.

They were looking at a bunch of townhomes, and Hyde lived in the second house from the end. They knocked on the door and patiently waited for someone to answer. They could hear a bunch of voices inside, some of which were children. After what seemed like an eternity, they knocked again. They still heard noises inside. Hall and Charlotte looked at each other, not knowing whether they were getting the brush off and should go, or whether they should keep waiting.

"Maybe they didn't hear us with all the noise," Charlotte said.

"There's a doorbell here," Hall said, pressing it.

Another minute later, an elderly woman answered the door. "Yes? Can I help you?"

"Yes, we're looking for Melvin Hyde," Hall replied.

"Are you with the police?"

"Umm, no, ma'am."

"Is he expecting you?"

"Uh, no, I don't believe so."

"Well, he's not here anyway."

"Please..." Hall said, putting his hand on the door before it closed.

"We're not here to hurt anybody," Charlotte said. "We just want to talk to him about something, something important, and then we'll be on our way."

"You're not looking for him for anything?" the woman asked, still a little dubious. Hyde's family was always skeptical about people knocking and looking for Melvin. If it wasn't the police after him, there were a half dozen other people that were looking to hurt him. Or looking to get him involved in some scheme that would land them in prison. Hyde's family tried to look out for him.

"Promise," Charlotte said. "We just wanna ask him if he knows a guy we're looking for and then we'll be gone."

The woman looked out into the street, seeing if there were any other strangers nearby. Since she didn't see anybody, her instincts told her they weren't lying or playing games.

"Wait here, I'll get him."

"Thank you."

Hall and Charlotte looked at each other again.

"You're welcome."

"For what?" Hall asked.

"Getting him."

"Oh, you think you're the reason why?"

"Of course."

"Ha!"

"Well, she was about to close the door on you," Charlotte said. "You probably frightened her."

"Me?! I frightened her? What about you?"

Charlotte flashed him a smile. "Does this look like the face anybody could be frightened of?"

Hall thought long and hard about answering. It sounded like one of those trick questions to him. If he answered incorrectly, he could have been sleeping on the couch by himself for a long time.

"Uh, no, definitely not. You have the face of an angel."

"Awe, thanks, sweetie." Charlotte gave him a quick peck on the lips before Hyde came to the door.

"And she would have closed the door on anybody, not just me."

"I dunno. If it wasn't for my sweet, innocent looks, we might not have gotten anything."

Hall was about to give a comeback, but then the door opened with Hyde standing there. "My grandmother said you wanted to see me about something?"

"Yeah, we wanted to ask you a couple of questions about a man named Walter Thurmond."

Hyde shook his head. "I don't know anybody named that."

Hall's shoulders slumped. He couldn't believe what he was hearing. "Really? You don't know him?"

"Nope. I do not."

"That's strange, because the police say that you do."

"You guys cops?"

Dark Day

"No, we're not," Charlotte answered. "We just wanna talk to you. Honestly."

"But that doesn't mean the police don't know we're here," Hall said. "And since we're talking honestly, if you don't talk to us, I know a Detective Bradham who will be here in thirty minutes if you choose to ignore us or feed us a bunch of lies."

"What are you guys? Rookies or something?"

"We're just private investigators working on a case. But like I said, the police are the ones who gave us your name, so if you don't talk to us, you're gonna have to talk to them. And I'm guessing that you don't wanna do that."

Hyde put his hand over his mouth and rubbed his lips. Then he looked out into the street, also looking for other strangers. "What are you guys asking about Thurmond for?"

"We believe he's involved in a murder."

"A murder? Which one?"

Hall and Charlotte looked at each other, hardly believing their ears. Hyde basically confirmed that the man was involved in multiple murders.

"Well, we're talking about Carly Learson," Charlotte said. "You know her?"

"Carly? Yeah, I know her. I mean, who doesn't? A lot of guys know her, and some in more ways than one, if you know what I mean."

"What way did you know her?" Hall asked.

Hyde shrugged only one of his shoulders. "Ahh, I

mean, I did a little business with her a time or two. Mostly small-time stuff, fencing something here or there, know what I mean?"

"You know she was involved with Thurmond?"

Hyde shrugged one of his shoulders again. "Ahh, like I said, she was involved with a lot of guys. I know they knew each other, but whether they were doing business together, I couldn't say."

"When was the last time you saw either of them?"

"Eh, Carly must have been about two, maybe three months ago."

"And Thurmond?" Charlotte asked.

"Ahh, I dunno... maybe... six, eight months ago, something like that."

Hall and Charlotte looked at each other, not quite believing his story. What he'd said about Learson seemed all right, but he'd hesitated a bit with his answer about Thurmond. Almost as if he was trying to think of the right lie.

"You wanna try that again?" Hall asked. "Hey, all we want is the truth here, then we'll be out of your hair."

Hyde looked out at the street again, as if he were specifically looking for someone. "Man, why don't you guys just bug off. You standing here is bad for my image, you know?"

"We could talk inside if you prefer."

"Are you kidding? Nobody comes inside. Especially to talk business. I got a mom, grandmom, girlfriend, and kids in there. They will throw all of us out if we go in there talking business. That's one of the rules of the house. Whatever I do, I do outside."

Hall reached into his pocket and removed some money. Charlotte's eyes almost bulged out of her head as she saw him handling it.

"What are you doing?" Charlotte asked.

Hall held the money out for Hyde to take. "There's fifty dollars here. Will that loosen your lips a little?"

Charlotte's eyes widened. "Fifty dollars? What are you doing?"

Hyde smiled, then took the money and counted it. "I don't know, man, I mean... fifty dollars is cool and all, but it sure would be nice for it to have some company if you know what I mean."

"Fifty's all I got on me." He then looked at Charlotte. "What about you?"

"Me?!"

"Yeah, you, c'mon. We have a chance to finally make some headway here, let's not be stingy now."

The tension on Charlotte's face was plainly evident and her jaw locked shut. She was obviously not happy about giving away their hard-earned money. She reluctantly opened her wallet and pulled out a twenty, holding it in the air.

"This is all that I have."

Hyde smiled again and snatched it from her fingers, putting the twenty on top of the other bills. "Eh, seventy's all right. I mean, a hundred would be better."

"It's all we got," Hall said. "Take it or leave it."

Hyde looked to his side, thinking of his kids inside. He was running short on funds, so even seventy dollars looked pretty good right about now. He'd probably have sold out his own mother for an extra thirty, but since Thurmond wasn't related, seventy would do. He looked out at the street again, causing both Hall and Charlotte to take a look back, wondering if they were missing something.

"You expecting someone?" Hall asked.

"Never know, man. Never know who might be watching."

"Who would be watching?" Charlotte asked.

"Like I said, you never know."

"Seems like you're kind of paranoid."

"Yo, you can call it whatever you want. You wanna call it paranoid, maybe it is, but it's what's kept me alive all these years. Always assume the worst, and you'll never be surprised when it actually happens."

Charlotte scrunched her face and looked at her boyfriend. "You know, that actually almost makes sense to me."

"As fascinating as your life philosophy may be, I didn't give you that seventy dollars for nothing," Hall said. "I am expecting to get something substantial out of that."

Hyde kept looking at the street and made a painful expression. "Let's go over to the side here and talk."

Hyde stepped outside and closed the door behind

him. He led his visitors down the steps and walked to the edge of the townhomes, going to the side of the building. Once all three seemed to be out of sight, Hyde took another peek around the edge of the building.

"You sure are a careful man," Hall said.

"Like I keep saying, it pays to be careful. You know all those guys who walk around carefree like they ain't got a worry in the world? They're the ones that wind up dead in a ditch somewhere with their pants around their ankles."

"Certainly an impressive image," Charlotte said.

"Call it whatever you want, I'm just saying."

"Can we get to Walter Thurmond now?" Hall asked.

"Yeah, Walt, sure. What do you wanna know?"

"Well, where we can find him for starters. He doesn't exactly list himself in the Yellow Pages."

"Yellow Pages? What's that?"

Hall shook his head. "Never mind. It's an old-time thing."

"Oh. Yeah, well, if you wanna find Walt, then you need to find out who his lady friend is at the time."

"New one every week?"

"Ahh, I wouldn't say every week. He rotates."

"He rotates?" Charlotte asked.

"Yeah, you know, Suzy this month, Mary next month, Charlene the month after, then Darlene, then Frita, then back to Suzy, Mary again, Charlene…"

"We get the picture."

"Yeah, well, that's kind of what he does. No one steady for a long period of time, but they're still regulars, too, sorta."

"That's so gross," Charlotte said.

"Call it what you want. The ladies don't seem to mind."

"What kind of self-respecting woman would…"

Hall quickly cut his girlfriend off before she went off on too much of a tangent. "So who is it this month? Do you know?"

"Uh, lemme think for a minute," Hyde replied. "Last time I saw Walt was about two weeks ago. I think he had Charlene with him. Yeah, Charlene. So you can probably find him at her place."

"And where can we find her?"

Hyde took another peek around the corner to make sure nobody new had arrived. "Uh, she's usually hanging out at her apartment over on Elkins."

"You got a number?"

Hyde shook his head. "Nah, I never been there. I just know that's where the woman lives."

"Elkins?"

"Yeah, Elkins and Hoover."

"Charlene have a last name?"

"Uh, yeah, what is it? Harkins. Yeah, that's it. Harkins. Charlene Harkins."

"You and Thurmond get along pretty good?" Charlotte asked.

"Yeah, not too bad. We never really had any problems. Why?"

"Just wondering. It seems like you just gave him up pretty easily."

"Hey, it's nothing personal," Hyde said. "It's just business. Walt would understand."

"Yeah, I bet he would," Hall said.

"It's all about survival, man. My survival's more important than his survival."

"Spoken like a true friend."

"Hey, it's a dog-eat-dog world out there. You want information, I got it, as long as you're willing to pay for it. Like I said, it's just business."

"You're a true entrepreneur."

"Yo, the cops ain't gonna be here or nothing, are they?"

"No, your secrets are safe with us."

"Good deal, man, good deal."

"You know any other places Thurmond likes to hang out, just in case he's not with Charlene?"

"Yeah, I mean, there's a couple pool places, a few bars, places like that. I've talked business with him a few times in a neighborhood place called Jeannie's."

"Jeannie's?"

"Yeah, it's a little bar over on, uh, Perkins Street."

"Anything else you know about him?"

Hyde shrugged. "Not really. I mean, if you're wanting to know what he likes to eat for breakfast or the clothes he wears or what makes him tick and things like that, I'm not the guy for that. We weren't that close. We did a few deals, worked a few things, but that's about the end of it."

"If this information isn't right, I'll be back," Hall said. "And I'll be bringing the police with me."

"Hey, I'm telling ya, it's right. Ain't gotta worry about that."

"And if I find out that you called him and warned him we were coming, I'll be back. But I won't have the police with me if you catch my drift."

"Hey, ain't gotta worry about that neither. I'm all about business. I'm also about recognizing when it is beneficial for me to do business with someone."

"Is that so?"

"Like now for instance. I recognize that we might be able to do a little business in the future if the need arises."

"Think so?"

"You're a PI. You might have future cases where you might need some knowledge or to be pointed in the right direction. Having people in the know, in the right places, might be advantageous for you."

"I'm assuming you're recommending your own services?"

Hyde smiled. "Now if I'm giving you bad information now, you won't come back to me in the future, would you? I'm just laying the bread crumbs down, if you follow me."

"Oh, we follow."

"And I'm sure you'd just be doing these future things out of the goodness of your heart, right?" Charlotte asked.

"Well, listen, man, I mean, ma'am, we all gotta eat, right? Throw a few Benjamins my way, and I'll find out whatever you wanna know. If I know it, I'll tell ya. If I don't, I'll find out about it. That's how it works."

Hall nodded, realizing that it would be advantageous to have someone like Hyde on their contact list. A person like him could come in handy for various situations. As long as they had the money to give him since he wouldn't work for free. Hall patted Hyde on the shoulder.

"So if something comes up in the future... we'll keep you in mind."

"My man," Hyde said. "That's what I like to see. Everybody gets what they want. Happiness all around."

"Well, let us check out this information you gave us," Hall said. "And then we'll see how happy we are."

9

Hall and Charlotte immediately went to the apartment complex that Hyde had told them about. Charlotte was especially happy about seeing the place once they arrived.

"Oh my...." she said, staring at the building. "It actually looks... normal. There's nothing falling apart. At least on the outside."

"I think you need to see someone about this fascination you have with crumbling buildings."

Charlotte gave him a look, not really finding him amusing. "So how are we gonna find this apartment? There's probably a couple hundred places in there."

Hall thought about it for a few seconds. "And it's a cinch we can't just sit out here all day looking for them."

"Looks like each apartment has its own entrance,

so that's a plus. We don't have to go down any long, dirty corridors."

"Let's check out the mailboxes. Maybe they have names on them."

They got out of the car and went over to the cluster of mailboxes that were outside, looking to see if any of the names were printed on them. They weren't, though. Hall and Charlotte went back to their car and sat there for a few minutes.

"Why don't we just call Bradham and have him look it up?"

"Didn't really wanna get him involved until we know for sure what we have," Hall replied.

"Well, right now we don't have anything unless we find out what apartment Harkins is in."

"Good point."

Hall called Bradham and told them where they were and how they got there. The detective had just gotten back to his office when his phone rang.

"Charlene Harkins?" Bradham asked, typing the name into his computer.

"That's right."

"How'd you come to her?"

"I told you. One of the names on the list gave her up."

"Did you give money for this too?"

"Uh, I can neither confirm nor deny."

Bradham sighed and shook his head. "Brandon."

"Hey, it got us a start. Don't wanna hear it."

Though Bradham disagreed with the methods, his friend was right, it did get them a start. Assuming the information was good. "OK, here we go, Charlene Harkins, apartment P433."

"P433, got it. Does this woman happen to have some sort of record?"

"Afraid of getting your ass beat if you knock on her door?"

"Well, doesn't hurt to know who you're dealing with."

"Charlene Harkins, been arrested for prostitution, assault, battery, theft, drug violations, and some traffic citations."

"Oh, is that all?"

Bradham laughed. "Yeah, seems like a peach, don't she?"

"All right, well, I guess we'll go see if she's in and talk to her. Unless you wanna join in on the fun."

"No, I got a couple other cases pulling at me. Let me know how it goes."

"I will."

Hall put the phone away and looked at Charlotte. "P433 and Bradham's not coming, so it's all ours."

"Oh, great."

"What's the matter?"

"What if Thurmond's in there too?"

"Even better," Hall replied. "Then we don't have to search anymore."

"What if things get... heated?"

"Do you forget I know how to handle myself?"

"Well, you did lose that fight with Coulson."

Hall rolled his eyes and then got out of the car. "I'm never gonna hear the end of that."

Charlotte also got out of the car. "You have to admit, for as tough as you are, and all the funky moves that you know, it is kind of a big thing that someone else took you out."

"He didn't take me out. It's not as if he beat the crap out of me. He just got in a lucky shot."

"Oh, a lucky shot. That must be it."

"Can we drop this and get back to what we're here for?"

"I suppose."

The apartment complex was spread out amongst the grounds, with numerous buildings throughout. Each building had two floors. There was a lower unit on the ground floor, then another apartment on the second floor. Each unit had its own entrance. Though the P building that Charlene Harkins lived in wasn't directly in front of them, Hall and Charlotte decided to walk over to it. It was a beautiful day, with the sun shining bright, plus they didn't want to pull up right in front of Harkins' unit and have someone get nervous at the sight of them. They thought it better if they surprised Charlene, and possibly Thurmond if he was there. Once they got to the P building, Hall looked at the parking lot.

"Should've asked Bradham what kind of car she drives," Hall said.

Hall didn't want to take the time to call the detective again since they were only a few feet from Harkins' door. So they went up to the apartment and started knocking on the door. It surprisingly didn't take long for an answer. Less than twenty seconds later, the door opened, revealing a somewhat attractive woman. She was in her thirties, though it looked like she hadn't brushed her hair all day. Her clothes were a little wrinkled, and there was a strong smell of liquor coming from her. But she had a cute face.

"What do you want?"

"Uh, Charlene?" Hall asked.

"Yeah, who are you?"

"I was actually looking for Walter, is he here?"

"You a friend of his?"

"Well, no, not really. I was looking to make a deal with him, and I was told he might be here."

"Who told you that?"

"Uh, I don't remember his name. I had a pretty sweet score lined up, and I was told Walter was the guy who could help me with it. Is he in?"

"No, he's not."

"You're his girl, right?"

"Sometimes."

"Could I leave my name and have him contact me later?" Hall asked.

"Uh, I suppose."

"Do you expect him later?"

"I dunno. Walt comes and goes. I never know when he's gonna show up."

"Well, if he wants in on this deal, tell him he's gotta let me know in the next three days. We're talking about a two-million-dollar score."

"Two million?"

"That's right. And the job's going down soon, so I need to know if he wants in. I've heard he's good at getting rid of certain things in a timely fashion."

"Walt's the best."

"That's why I want him."

Harkins looked at Charlotte. "Who's she?"

"Oh, her? She's my old lady."

"You can do better."

"Excuse me?" Charlotte replied.

"No offense, honey, but you don't exactly look like you're cut out for this kind of business."

"I'm just fine, thank you."

"It takes a hard woman to hook up with a man that's involved in this type of work. Do yourself a favor, go find yourself a man who's got a nine-to-five job and hang on to him. Leave this life in the dust."

Charlotte put her hands on Hall's arm. "I think I'll stick with him a while."

Harkins shook her head. "Trust me, kid, I was just like you fifteen years ago. Look at me now. Believe me when I tell you, run."

"Can we get back to our business now?" Hall said. "I got two million on the line in the next few days."

"What'd you say the job was?"

"That's my bag. I just need to know whether Thurmond wants in. You got something I can write my number on?"

"Uh, yeah, hold on."

Harkins left to grab a piece of paper as Hall removed his pen.

"You believe her?" Charlotte asked, getting a little steamed.

Hall laughed at how mad she looked. "Relax, it's fine."

"Fine for you. She just told me—"

The door opened up again, making Charlotte closer her mouth quickly. Charlene handed Hall an index card. Hall put his name and phone number on it and handed it back to her.

"Remember, I need an answer from him quickly."

"I'll tell him if he checks in," Harkins replied.

Hall and Charlotte then started walking back to the car.

"Do you believe her?" Charlotte asked.

"She was just trying to look after you, apparently."

"Saying I don't have what it takes."

"That's not technically what she said."

"Might as well be. Meant the same thing."

"I'm the one that should be offended," Hall said.

"How so?"

"She told you to leave me."

"Well, that I could understand."

Hall laughed. "Oh really?"

"Yeah, I mean, it is kind of understandable. You're not exactly my type."

"Oh, I'm not, huh?"

"Yeah, I'm usually with the prettier type of men."

Hall looked at her and shook his head. Then they both started laughing as they hugged and clung to each other, continuing their walk back to the car. Once they got to the car, Hall started it up, then drove around to the P building, making sure they had a good vantage point of apartment 433.

"What are you doing?" Charlotte asked.

"Watching."

"For what?"

"Thurmond."

"You just gave your phone number for him to call. Why don't you just wait at home for it?"

"Yeah, but who says he's gonna?" Hall said. "He doesn't know me. Maybe he'll pass."

"On two million dollars? Seems like that's enough to pique his interest."

"Hopefully. Depends how careful he is."

While they were waiting, Hall called Bradham again, just to keep him updated and let him know what was going on.

"And who's to say he's not there already?" Hall asked.

"Good point. Maybe he has her answer the door for everyone, and she feels them out."

"In any case, we don't have much else to do anyway besides wait here."

"For how long?"

"As long as it takes."

10

They'd been sitting on Harkins' apartment for the past three days. They hadn't seen one sign of Thurmond in the time they'd been there. All day, all night, from the early morning, until well after midnight.

"I think we're wasting our time here," Charlotte said. "He's not showing up."

"He's gotta show up at some point."

"No, he doesn't. He might have moved on to the next girl on his list. And you haven't gotten a call yet either. I think it's safe to assume he's not interested."

"Could just be taking his time."

"On two million dollars? How many people would just be taking their time?"

"People who are careful about not getting caught," Hall replied.

"Brandon, just admit that this isn't going to work."

"I'm not ready to go there yet."

"When are you going to be ready?"

"Let's just give it another day or two."

Hall and Charlotte were back at it the next night, though she believed it was still a waste of time. Considering they didn't really have any other leads to go on yet, Hall didn't mind, though he did wish Thurmond would hurry and show up. He didn't want to admit it to his girlfriend, but he was getting tired of sitting there with nothing to show for it too. Once again, they spent the entire day there, and it looked like it was going to be another time sink. But once darkness set in, that's when things started to get interesting. They noticed several people going to Harkins' apartment, though none of them looked like Thurmond. A couple were wearing hats or hoodies, so it was tough to make out their faces, but Hall and Charlotte were fairly confident that none were the guy they were looking for. Six men and one woman went into the apartment, and roughly thirty minutes later, none of them had left.

"What do you think that's all about?" Charlotte asked. "What are they doing in there?"

Hall barely turned his head to look at her, but raised one of his eyebrows. "You really wanna know?"

Charlotte immediately got his meaning. "Ew, that's disgusting. Don't even say that."

Hall laughed. "Well, you asked."

"Yeah, but, ew, no."

"It's possible, I guess. Though that's a lot of people to be getting down and dirty in that place."

"Ew, just stop, just… stop. I don't even wanna think about that." Charlotte then shivered, trying to get the images out of her system.

"So I take it that you don't want us to ever get into the swinging lifestyle?"

Charlotte glared at him. "Are you not happy enough with just me?"

Hall laughed again. "I'm just teasing. Don't burn a hole through me yet."

"You don't really think that's what they're doing in there, do you?"

Hall shrugged. "Beats me. Could be doing the hanky panky. Could be playing cards. Or maybe they're all waiting for Thurmond to show up. Maybe he's got some deal going on."

"I really hope it's the last option."

"You wanna go up and peek through the windows?"

"No!"

They didn't have to wait too much longer to learn what it was, though. Another car pulled up, right in front of Harkins' apartment. A man got out, and Hall immediately started taking pictures of him as he walked up to the apartment and went inside. Once he was out of sight, Hall and Charlotte looked at the photos.

"That's him!" Charlotte excitedly said.

"That it is."

"It's about time."

"So I'm assuming they're talking business in there," Hall said. "Thurmond must have something going on that he needs all of them for."

"How you wanna handle this?"

"No need to go barging in or anything. Let them do their business, wait for everyone to leave, see what happens after that."

"What's the matter? Afraid of taking them all on by yourself?"

"No, I'm not afraid."

"Still got that beating Coulson gave you in the back of your mind?"

Hall rolled his eyes. He really was never going to live that down. "No, I don't have it in the back of my mind, and it wasn't a beating. He gave me a shot to the stomach, and then one to the back of my neck. That's not a beating."

"Well, you were on the ground."

"I slipped."

"Uh huh."

"And anyway, regardless of that, barging in there and taking on eight people isn't exactly my idea of being smart."

"There's nine in there, not eight."

"Whatever."

"And if you want some backup, I could always run

into the kitchen real quick and look for the frying pans."

Hall smiled. "Nice. Great idea."

This time it was Charlotte doing the laughing. "Hey, just trying to help since you are apparently needing more of it these days. Maybe I should take the lead."

Hall stared straight ahead, not really enjoying the ribbing, though he wasn't offended by it either. "Are you done?"

"Uh, yeah, I guess so."

"He did not take me out."

Charlotte smiled. "That really bothers you, doesn't it?"

"No, it doesn't."

"Then why'd you bring it up?"

"Because you brought it up."

"But you brought it up just now."

Hall put his hands up. "OK, can we just drop it now?"

"Consider it dropped."

They both stared at the apartment for a few more minutes, seeing no other activity.

"Seriously, what are we going to do after this?" Charlotte asked.

"Guess it depends on them."

"How so?"

"Well, if they all leave and Thurmond stays there, I guess we start knocking on the door."

"And if he leaves along with them?"

"Then I guess we follow him," Hall answered.

They waited another hour before they saw any life from the apartment. The door finally opened, and the visitors left one by one. They counted the number of people leaving to make sure they didn't forget anybody in case they had to go in. Everyone was accounted for. They waited a few more minutes to see if Thurmond came back out, plus, they didn't want to go in right after the other people had left. Looked kind of fishy that way, Hall thought.

"Now?" Charlotte asked, twenty minutes after the visitors had left.

Hall looked at her and nodded. "Now."

They drove closer to the apartment so they didn't have as far to walk, then got out and went up to the door. Charlotte had a nasty-looking expression on her face.

"What?" Hall asked.

"What if they really are doing something now?"

"Would you like your innocent angel eyes to sit in the car and wait for me?"

"No. I'll survive."

They knocked on the door, but there was no answer. They continued knocking until they finally heard someone moving inside.

"All right, all right, I'm coming!" Harkins yelled.

She opened the door, standing there in a short, revealing silk purple robe. It was tied, but barely covered her essentials, and still revealed quite a bit of cleavage.

"Oh, it's you again. You caught me at a bad time. Or a good time depending on your point of view."

Hall and Charlotte did everything they could to not glance down at her ample breasts and tanned legs.

"Is, uh, uh" Hall said, forgetting Thurmond's name. He looked to Charlotte for help.

"Walter Thurmond?" Charlotte said, nodding at him.

"Oh yeah. That's him. Is he here?"

"Uh, you really caught us at a bad time," Harkins said. "Can you come back later?"

"I really can't. I need an answer now from him one way or the other."

Harkins sighed, looking disappointed. "Just when I was about to…"

Hall cut her off, not wanting to hear any disturbing details about their plans. "If you go get him now, maybe another night when he's not here, we can come back for a little extra something."

Harkins looked at the both of them and smiled. "Now that I could get behind."

Charlotte's eyes almost popped out of her head upon hearing what her boyfriend said. She turned her head and looked at him, not believing it. Hall could feel her eyes upon him.

"I can't believe you just said that."

"Relax," Hall said. "I only said it to give her another reason to go get him."

"I'm sure there could've been another thing to say that would've accomplished that."

"Maybe so. But not as fast," Hall smiled. Charlotte shook her head, still not liking it. "Besides, it's not like we're ever gonna be back here after tonight anyway."

"And if by some cruel, cruel joke we are?"

"Then I can always say I pulled a muscle… somewhere."

Charlotte stared at the door and shook her head again. "We have to work on the way you make plans."

A minute later, the door opened again, Thurmond standing there. He was dressed in pants and shoes, but no shirt.

"So you're the guy who dropped by the other day, Char said?"

"Yep," Hall replied.

"Some type of deal you got lined up?"

"Yeah, there's two million on the line."

"I got your number. I'll call you tomorrow."

"I really need to know now."

Thurmond leaned forward. "I'm a little busy right now, you know? Leave your number and I'll get back to you."

"It's either now or not at all."

"I'm afraid I'll have to pass on it then," Thurmond said, attempting to close the door.

Hall put his arm up to block it, successfully

preventing it from slamming shut in his face. The two men struggled by the door for a few seconds until Thurmond realized he was losing the battle. He then ran towards the bedroom, Hall rushing inside after him. Charlotte went inside too, to make sure that Charlene wasn't a problem. Thurmond ran into the bedroom, followed closely by Hall, who had almost caught up to him by then. Thurmond jumped across the bed, rolling over onto the other side, trying to get to the table next to it so he could reach his gun. Just as Thurmond opened the drawer, Hall flew across the bed, landing on top of Thurmond as they both went crashing into the wall. They got up simultaneously, Thurmond reaching for the drawer again. Hall slammed it shut, then delivered a left cross to Thurmond's face, making him fall back on the bed. Hall reached over to pick his opponent up, but Thurmond put his feet on Hall's stomach and flipped him over, landing on the other side of the bed.

Once again, Thurmond rushed to the table for his gun. Hall quickly got back to his feet and jumped over the bed again, the two men wrestling against the wall. Hall pulled Thurmond away from the table as they started throwing punches. Hall was doing most of the work, though. Thurmond got in one or two shots, but Hall was blocking most of them. After a few minutes, Hall was able to get the upper hand, using his punches and kicks to finally subdue his adversary. Ultimately, Hall delivered a punch that decisively ended the conflict, sending Thurmond crashing to the ground. Thurmond hit his head on the frame of the bed as he went down, causing a little gash on the side of his head. Charlotte and Charlene were looking on at the festivities in the frame of the door, and Thurmond's girlfriend wasn't looking too pleased at what she was witnessing.

"What do you think you're doing?!" Charlene yelled.

Hall didn't pay her much attention and instead focused on getting Thurmond taken care of. Hall dragged the man over to the wall, making sure there was nothing in arm's reach that he could use for a weapon. Charlene continued yelling at Hall, who still wasn't paying any attention to her. Charlotte was, though, and she was starting to get ticked off.

"Would you just pipe down?!" Charlotte yelled.

"I will not pipe down! Did you see what he just did?! Did you see what your boyfriend just did?!"

"I saw! Now shut up!"

"I will not shut up!"

True to her word, Charlene didn't quiet down. Instead, she was getting more and more agitated with each passing second. Eventually, she grew tired of Hall not listening to her and didn't like what was going on in her apartment, so she decided to do something about it to try to help her boyfriend out. She ran over to Hall and jumped on his back, her robe completely falling off in the process, not that she seemed to notice or care. She was completely naked on his back as she tried to wrestle him away. Thurmond was still holding his head, though, and didn't have much energy to try another attack.

After a minute of wrestling, Thurmond finally decided he was going to give it another shot. Just as he got to his feet, Hall flipped Charlene over his shoulder, the woman landing hard on the floor. Seeing Thurmond up again, Hall reached back and gave him another powerful shot that landed right across his jaw, sending him sprawling to the floor again. Charlotte walked into the room shaking her head, looking at the naked woman on the floor.

"Some people just don't learn," she said.

Hall looked at his girlfriend and shrugged. Charlotte went over to the woman and grabbed her by the arm to help her back up. She grabbed Charlene's robe and handed it to her, not that she seemed all that upset or modest at standing there with nothing on. Charlene angrily put the robe back on and stood in front of Hall.

"If you think this is over, you got another thing coming, mister! I'm not gonna let you stand here and get away with this, you know!"

Charlotte rolled her eyes, wondering how stupid some people could get. "Would you please shut up and sit down?" She actually said it nicely this time, hoping it would finally sink in.

"No!" Charlene shouted. She also started pointing her finger in Hall's face.

"Ma'am, please sit down," Hall said, keeping his cool. He wasn't going to hit the woman no matter what she did, but he was getting a little annoyed at how animated she was.

"You can't silence me! You might think you're able to run roughshod over everyone else, but I'm not gonna stand for it, do you hear me?!"

"Unfortunately."

Charlotte, who didn't get mad easily, had now lost any semblance of patience. "Sit down!"

"No," Charlene replied. "What are you gonna do about it? You can't make me."

Charlotte begged to differ and was going to prove it. She didn't need a frying pan this time. The anger had been slowly building up inside and now it was boiling over. Taking a page out of Hall's book, she reached back with her right hand, then uncorked a robust shot across Charlene's face, instantly knocking her to the floor. Charlene stayed on the ground, her robe flying open to expose her breasts once again as she held the side of her face. She now shut up, though. Hall looked at his girlfriend, surprised at her actions, though impressed.

"I didn't think you had it in you," Hall said.

Charlotte almost looked embarrassed at what she had done. "Yeah, well, there's only so much a person can take listening to that. And I've had enough!"

Hall looked down at Charlene, appreciating the

quiet. "Apparently so has she. You wanna call Bradham and tell him to come down?"

"What about them?"

"It's fine. I don't think they're gonna give us any more problems, right?" Hall asked, looking down at them, though he didn't expect a reply, and he didn't get one.

Charlotte went into the other room and called Bradham to tell him what was going on. She got through to the detective right away, who immediately dispatched a couple of patrol units to their location. She came back into the bedroom after talking to Bradham to let Hall know what was going on.

"He's got a couple units coming over now."

"Good," Hall said. "What about him?"

"He said he'll meet us down at the station. The cops coming over would bring them down for questioning."

Hall nodded. "Sounds like a plan. He say how long the cops would take to get here?"

"Probably two or three minutes."

"I don't think that should be a problem." Hall looked at Thurmond and Charlene, both of whom were still on the floor holding their heads. "Doesn't look like these two are going anywhere."

A police car showed up a few minutes later, then another one about thirty seconds after that. Hall explained what had happened, though Bradham had already told the officers that a PI was there and in control of the situation. After the officers had put the suspects in their patrol cars, one of the officers turned to Hall.

"Bradham said he wanted you guys to come down to the station too."

Hall nodded. "We'll follow you down."

As Hall and Charlotte walked back to their car, she noticed a little bit of blood on his hand.

"You OK?"

Hall noticed her eyes focused on his hand, and then he looked at it. "Oh, it's nothing. He wiped the blood off on his pants, revealing a little cut on one of his knuckles. "No big deal." Hall and Charlotte then looked at each other in a loving manner. "I'm proud of that right hand you threw in there."

"Just taking lessons from you."

"Keep that up and you might be able to take me out one day."

"Doesn't seem so hard," Charlotte said. "I mean, everyone else is doing it these days."

"Really? We're really gonna keep that up? After I just took him out in there? That should redeem me."

Charlotte smiled at him. "Nope. You're not living that down for a long, long time."

11

Once they got to the police station, they were immediately greeted by Bradham. He asked how everything went down, and Hall and Charlotte explained it in great detail.

"They're saying you guys assaulted them," Bradham said.

"What?!" Charlotte replied. "That's crazy. We did not!"

Bradham put his hands up to calm them down. "We're already dismissing those claims. Thurmond had a gun that he was reaching for, so we're chalking it up as self-defense. Though a really good lawyer could probably argue that he was reaching for the gun because you were chasing him, but we'll leave that for another time."

"What jerks!"

"And you punching Harkins... probably a little dicey as well."

"She climbed on his back, was wagging her finger in his face, what was I supposed to do?"

"Yeah, but the way she tells it, that was a few minutes before you cold-cocked her."

"I thought she was about to go after him," Charlotte said.

Bradham smiled. "Yeah, well, we're dismissing her claim as well. They're both in a lot of hot water, and neither of them is gonna press the issue. But I want you both to know they could if they really wanted to. That's why I say you guys gotta be careful about doing this stuff. You can have the best of intentions and think you're in the right, and still get jammed up in a lot of trouble."

Hall nodded. "We'll be more careful."

"I'm gonna have a crack at them in the interview room. You guys can watch through the glass if you want."

"Both at the same time?"

"No, we'll talk to Thurmond first, then Harkins. We'll see what they know, who they know, and what they're willing to give up."

"I'm surprised they're willing to talk," Charlotte said.

"Neither has asked for an attorney, so we'll see how it goes," Bradham said. The detective then pointed out a room down the hall. "Just head over to that door, there's another detective inside. I already told him to expect you so just sit in there and watch."

Hall and Charlotte did as their friend suggested and went into the room with the other detective to watch Bradham interview the suspects. The room had windows on two walls, as interview rooms were on both sides of it. Bradham took on Thurmond first, questioning him for almost thirty minutes. Thurmond didn't say much, so Bradham went to the other room to talk to Harkins. She didn't say much either. Although in her case, it was because she really didn't know very much. Thurmond didn't usually include her in any plans he was making because he thought she had loose lips. Bradham didn't question her for as long, realizing she didn't have much information to share. After leaving the interview room, Bradham went to visit the other detective to see what he thought so far.

"He obviously knows what's going on," Bradham said.

"No doubt," the other detective replied.

"He doesn't seem like he's gonna give it up, though."

"How 'bout you play them off against each other?" Hall asked.

"That only works if they both know something, and they both know the other one knows something. If she knows nothing, and he knows that, it's not gonna work."

"You can't make it seem like she does?"

"How am I gonna do that?"

Hall shrugged. "I dunno. You're the professional interrogator. We know he's involved in some type of insurance scam, and we got a dead body. Is there any reason why she might not have overheard something she wasn't supposed to?"

Bradham thought about it for a few seconds. After discussing it with the other detective, along with Hall and Charlotte putting in their two cents, Bradham thought he might have come up with something. He went back into the room with Thurmond and sat down across from him.

"You wanna let me out of here now?"

Bradham adjusted his tie. "We still have some things to go over."

"I already told you, man. I don't know anything about anything about anything."

"That's not what your girlfriend says."

"She don't know anything either."

Bradham held his legal pad up in the air. Thurmond saw the whole page had writing on it. "That's what she's told me so far."

"She couldn't have."

"Oh, she did."

"I don't even talk that much business around her."

"Really? And the five guys and one woman who were at the apartment tonight? Just visiting?"

Thurmond sighed and put his elbow on the table, holding his head up with his hand. "That dumb bitch."

"We also know you knew Carly Learson," Bradham said. "You were seen arguing outside her apartment a couple weeks ago."

"Whoa, if you're thinking I'm the one who killed her, you are way off base."

"Evidence is pointing your way."

"I don't care what evidence you got. I didn't do it."

"I already know what's going on. I just need you to fill in the missing pieces."

"I told you, I don't know nothing."

"I've got three murders on my hands right now and guess who's looking good for it?" Bradham said, staring at his suspect.

The piercing eyes made Thurmond uncomfortable. "I told you I didn't do it. And what do you mean three?"

"Carly Learson. Wendy Groshens ring a bell? Don't tell me you didn't know her. I already know the scheme you and Carly were working on."

Thurmond rolled his eyes. "I didn't kill Groshens either."

"So you admit you knew her?"

"I mean, I knew... wait, who's the third person?"

"Guy named Armstrong. Gonna tell me you don't know him either?"

"No, I'm serious, I don't know anybody named Armstrong. You ain't gonna try to pin that one on me. Who the hell is that?"

"He was having an affair with Groshens."

"An affair? Man, I don't know nothing about that. Don't even know who that guy is."

"So tell me what you do know," Bradham said, leaning back in his chair, looking relaxed. "Make me believe that you didn't kill these two women."

"Why should I get myself in deeper?"

"You're already deeper! If you're not responsible for killing these women, you can get yourself out of this mess by telling me what you know. You wanna go down for two murders you didn't do? 'Cause that's where this is heading if you don't come clean."

Thurmond sighed and rubbed his face. "All right, all right, I didn't kill those girls."

"So who did?"

"I dunno, it was… above me."

"What do you mean above you?"

"OK, so we were working this scheme…"

"The insurance bit?"

"No, no, not yet. That came later. Me and Carly, and a few other people, we were hitting businesses and people up, taking a few things here and there, if you know what I mean, then selling them, things like that."

"You were stealing and then fencing? Just say what it is. Don't dance around it."

"OK, so that's what we were doing. Then some guy contacted me out of the blue, asked if we wanted to work a big gig, that we were just messing around with some small-time stuff doing what we were doing. This was some big money."

"What's this guy's name?"

"Jack."

"Jack what?"

"Ripper."

Bradham looked at him like he was crazy. "Jack Ripper? C'mon."

"What?"

"Jack Ripper?"

"What, that's the guy's name."

"Jack the Ripper?"

"Jack the Ripper? Who's that?" Thurmond asked. "That the same guy?"

"You never heard of him?"

"Nah. Jack the Ripper, who's that? We talkin' about the same guy?"

Bradham leaned on the table, putting his index and middle fingers against his temple. "I wouldn't think so."

"Yeah, anyway, Ripper asks if we wanna work this thing he's got going on. Some big insurance scam. Me and Carly said yeah. The other people we were hanging around with didn't wanna do it. So me and Carly did."

"How long was this going on?"

"Maybe a couple months. Two, three months, something like that."

"So what was going on? Fake accidents?"

"Yeah, accidents, phony thefts, like paintings, jewelry, accident claims, the whole works."

"And what, Groshens eventually found out about it, so you had to kill her?"

"What? No! No, nothing like that. Wendy was in on it, man."

Bradham raised his eyebrows, surprised to hear it. "She was in on it?"

"Yeah."

"How'd you manage that?"

"I dunno. She was already on the inside when we were brought on board."

"Who did that?"

"I guess Ripper did. He was the one that introduced us."

Bradham rubbed his forehead, trying to wrap his head around everything. "So Ripper brings all of you guys on?"

"Yeah."

"And how much money are we talking here?"

"Me and Carly probably pulled in about twenty thousand each."

Bradham leaned back in his chair again, thinking. "Twenty thousand?"

"That's right."

"How much did the others get?"

"I don't know. We just put in the claims, then we got paid for each job."

"How many other people were involved in this?"

"Nobody that I know of."

"And who paid you?"

"I'd meet up with Wendy, and she'd give us our share."

"What about Ripper?" Bradham asked.

"After the first two or three times, I never saw him again. He'd call me by phone a few times, but never face to face after those initial meetings."

Bradham tapped his fingers on the desk as he tried to figure out what was going on. "So when you were seen arguing with Carly outside her apartment, what was that about?"

"She wanted more money. She thought we weren't making enough money from the gig, and she was asking for more."

"And you didn't?"

"Listen, would I have liked a bigger cut? Sure, man, who wouldn't? I mean, the things we were doing, I'm sure was a lot more valuable than the twenty grand we got from it. But it wasn't our bag. It was somebody else's scheme. I mean, it was pretty easy work. I told her to just shut up and be grateful the money was coming in."

"I take it she didn't listen?"

"She was telling anyone who would listen that she wanted more money. One time on the phone I was talking to Ripper, she took the phone from me and started yacking on him, telling him we wanted more. Then if we met with Wendy, she told her we wanted a bigger cut. Then she started telling other people we knew about the scheme, people who weren't even involved in it."

"So she was disgruntled and letting people know she was disgruntled?"

"Yeah."

"So you think that's why she was killed?"

Thurmond shrugged. "I mean, who knows, right? You know the old saying, loose lips sinks ships. I told her she needed to button it up, but she was insistent."

"So maybe Ripper got tired of dealing with the mess and killed Learson. Why would Groshens get killed?"

"I dunno, beats me. Maybe she wanted a bigger cut too. Or maybe Ripper got tired of dealing with it all and wanted to tie it off."

"So why wouldn't he kill you too?"

"I dunno. Maybe he thought I was good to go and wouldn't talk. Or maybe he wanted to use me for something else. One thing, man, when I got a good gig going on, I don't make waves. And I don't bite the hand that feeds me."

"Or maybe he just didn't get around to you yet," Bradham said. Thurmond shrugged, not having an answer. "What about Remi Coulson? You know him?"

"Remi?" Thurmond stared at the table as he thought. "Nah, doesn't ring a bell."

Bradham took out Coulson's picture and put it on the table. "How 'bout this guy?"

Thurmond picked it up and looked at it. "Uh… yeah… yeah, I know him."

"That's Remi Coulson."

"Nah, that's not the name I know."

"What do you know him as?"

"Dave... Smith, or Jones, or Adams, something like that."

"How do you know him?"

"The uh... second time I talked with Ripper, this guy was there. Standing in the background. Didn't say much. Didn't say anything, actually. Looked like he was just there for muscle. You know, gotta have the intimidation thing going on."

"What about after that?"

Thurmond shook his head. "Nah, never seen him again after that."

"You're sure?"

"Never saw Ripper again after that."

"Maybe you saw him somewhere else?"

Thurmond continued racking his brain. "It's funny... you know, I thought I might have seen him somewhere else once, but I thought I was just seeing things."

"Where else?"

"This one time I met with Wendy for her to give us our payment. It was the three of us. Me, Wendy, and Carly. We were in the park, sitting on the bench. We got up to leave, and I thought there was a guy sitting in a parked car across from us, you know, looking at us. But he turned his head away real quick and then drove off. For a second it looked like that guy, Smith, Jones,

Coulson, whoever he is, but I couldn't be sure. But it looked like it might have been him. Couldn't be positive, though."

"You know where to find this guy?"

Thurmond shook his head. "Couldn't tell ya. Don't know."

"You know anyone else who might know him?"

"Nope. Only people I knew in this operation were Wendy, Carly, and Ripper."

"And two of them are dead."

"Like I said, it wasn't me."

"You know what day that was?" Bradham asked. "When you were in the park and saw that guy?"

"Uh, it was a… Thursday, I think. No, it was a Friday. I remember 'cause Wendy mentioned something about weekend plans. It was a Friday afternoon, maybe two or three weeks ago."

"What kind of car?"

"I don't know. Four-door sedan. Red. Didn't see a make or anything."

Bradham talked with his suspect for another twenty minutes, going over everything again to make sure Thurmond didn't change his tune. Once he was done, and the story matched up again, Bradham finished the interrogation and went back into the middle room.

"What do you think?" Bradham asked.

"Sounds like he's telling the truth to me," the detective answered.

"Yeah, I think so too."

"It's a shame he didn't know more about Coulson," Charlotte said.

"That's OK," Bradham said. "We can still try to run him down."

"How?"

"We know he was near the park on a Friday a couple weeks ago. We go through the camera footage from everything near there, see if we get a hit. If we can get a hit on the plate, we might be in business."

"And if you can't?"

Bradham made a painful-looking expression. "Then we might be back to square one."

12

Bradham and some of his colleagues spent the better part of a day going through all the footage they had of the area near the park where Coulson had been spotted. They eventually found the car that matched the red vehicle that Thurmond had told them about.

"There it is," Bradham said, pointing to it on his screen.

The car had gone through a red light a few streets over from the park.

"Got a nice clear picture of the license plate," another detective said.

"Bet you it's a rental."

"No bet."

They typed the plate into their computer and immediately got back a hit.

"Glad I didn't bet," Bradham said.

"What, it's not a rental?"

"Nope."

"Stolen?"

"Eh, I dunno. Comes back to an Erin O'Malley."

"Who's she?"

"Looking her up now," Bradham said, typing her name into the computer. "Twenty-eight years old, no criminal record."

"She report her car stolen?"

"Not that I can tell. It's not in the system."

"Maybe she's a girlfriend?"

"Could be. That would make sense though, right? A guy like Coulson isn't going to want to leave a trail, renting cars, things like that. He's gonna want to try to stay hidden as much as possible."

"Maybe we should pay this girl a visit."

"Probably be a good idea to have a couple patrol cars nearby in case Coulson is actually there," Bradham said.

Bradham printed out the sheet with O'Malley's information on it and grabbed it as the two detectives rushed out of the room. They had a couple of patrol cars meet them at O'Malley's address. One met them in front of the house, and one was watching the back door, in case Coulson was in there and tried to escape upon seeing the police officers there. Bradham radioed everyone to make sure they were in position, and once he got confirmation that they were, they moved in.

"No red car in the driveway," the other detective said.

"I noticed," Bradham replied.

The detectives went up to the front door and knocked. O'Malley lived in a modest home in a middle-class neighborhood. It certainly was no mansion or anything, but the neighborhood was nice, and the house was a two-story colonial that looked like it had been kept up. After waiting for a minute, they got no response. Bradham put his ear up to the door to see if he could detect any movement inside. He heard nothing, though.

"Could be she's out working," his partner said.

"Could be." Bradham continued knocking loudly for another minute, hoping to draw some type of response. He didn't get one. He grabbed his radio. "Anybody seeing anything."

"Nothing," the officer watching the back replied.

Bradham turned the knob on the door, but it was locked. "I guess we'll have to sit on it."

The detectives walked away from the house and stood on the front lawn with the patrol officer that was stationed there, and they talked about their next move.

"Could just visit her at her work," the detective said.

"Yeah, we could," Bradham replied. "I really wanted to get a look inside that house."

"What for?"

"See if Coulson has actually been living there. That

would tell us how serious their relationship is or whether they actually have one."

As they were talking, the neighbor across the street came out of his house. He was an older gentleman, in his sixties, possibly seventies, but looked very athletic for his age. He looked like he could have given all of them a tumble and possibly come out victorious.

"You guys looking for something?"

"We're looking for Erin O'Malley," Bradham replied. "You know her?"

"Erin? Yeah, I know her. Nice girl. Very friendly."

"You know where she's at?"

"Is she in trouble?"

"Could be. That's why we wanna find her."

"I can't imagine Erin doing something."

"Well, it's not actually her. It's someone we think she knows."

"Oh. That dark-haired guy who's been hanging around here lately?"

Bradham looked at the other detective. "What dark-haired guy?" Bradham had a picture of Coulson in his pocket and took it out to show to the neighbor. "This the guy?"

The man nodded, pointing at the picture. "That's the guy. Doesn't seem all that friendly. Not really the type of guy I figured Erin would go for."

"Why's that?"

"Well, Erin is so nice and friendly, always with a warm smile when she walks the neighborhood. But this guy, every time I've seen him, he's got a permanent scowl on his face. Not friendly at all. Mean eyes."

"When was the last time you saw either of them?"

The neighbor rubbed his chin as he thought. "Must be four or five days. You know, it's funny, Erin's been here three or four years, and I've never gone more than two days without seeing her up to now."

"What do you mean, coming home from work? Things like that?"

"Yeah, and she would always take a walk around, usually every other day. It's strange that I haven't seen her lately. Haven't seen her car either."

"Could she have gone on vacation?"

"Hmm, it's not likely. The previous times she's gone on vacation, she always used a taxi to take her to the airport. Said she didn't like leaving her car there for an extended period of time."

"How long's this guy been hanging around?" Bradham asked.

"Probably about a month or so."

"Ever see him with his own car?"

The man shook his head. "Nah, never seen him with a car. Drove Erin's a lot, though."

"Ever talk to him?"

"One day they were walking along and I tried to strike up a conversation with him. No dice. He wasn't having it. She was friendly as could be, just like always. Him, though? Forget about it. He looked at me with these cold eyes, looked like he wanted to shoot me dead just for looking at him. Like I said, not friendly at all. They struck me as an odd couple."

"Ever hear any noises over there? Fights, banging, loud parties, anything like that?"

"No, can't say that I have. They were pretty quiet."

The detectives then heard the officer's voice from the back of the house come over their radio. "Got something back here. Might wanna come check it out."

The three police officers raced to the back of the house, Bradham telling the uniformed cop to stay out front to cover just in case someone was in there and came racing out. Bradham started peppering the officer with questions as soon as he saw him.

"Whatcha got?"

"Back door's open," the officer answered. "Plus, I looked through one of the windows and it looks like it's kind of messy."

Bradham took a look for himself through the window. It wasn't messy in the ordinary sense, where a place just needed some tidying up. It looked like the place had been ransacked.

"You said the back door's open?" Bradham asked.

"Yeah. Well, it's not open, but it's unlocked. I checked the handle already."

Bradham looked at his partner. "Looks to me like we got probable cause to go in."

The officers took their guns out and gathered around the door, Bradham taking the lead position. They opened the back door, which led into a little laundry room. With nothing there other than the usual washer, dryer, and a couple of wall cabinets, they went to the next door, which led to the inside part of the house. Bradham listened for any activity inside the house, but there was none. He turned the handle of the door, which was also unlocked. The officers proceeded through the door, slowly, aiming their guns in case they ran into Coulson, or whoever else might have been there. They stepped into the kitchen, which looked pretty normal, as any other kitchen would.

Bradham directed the uniformed officer to the left, to a small family room, which was where they'd initially seen the mess through the window. He and the other detective proceeded through the rest of the house. They entered the living room, which was also wrecked, magazines and papers all over the floor, a coffee table flipped on its side, and a few pillows thrown about. They checked out the other rooms downstairs, which consisted of a bedroom and a bathroom. Those two areas were clean, especially considering what the rest of the house looked like so far.

Bradham and his partner were rejoined by the other officer as the three of them went up the steps. Once they got to the top of the stairs, a bathroom was right in front of them, which they easily cleared. There was a bedroom door to both sides of them, and each was closed. Bradham took the one to the left, as the other two took the one to the right. They each opened the doors simultaneously upon going in. That was all the checking they needed to do, however. The bedroom was also a mess, just like the two rooms downstairs. The pillows and sheets were off the bed, a lamp and nightstand were knocked over, clothes on the floor, it was a wreck. But the biggest thing was what Bradham was looking at. He put his gun away and took a deep sigh as he stared. Erin O'Malley was lying there amongst the mess. He knelt down beside her to feel a pulse, even though he could already tell she was gone. He'd seen enough dead bodies to know by now. Sometimes it got to him. This was one of those times. He usually wasn't bothered by seeing the dead bodies of hardened criminals or people who had done really bad things. But seeing people who didn't have criminal records, or who were, by all accounts, good people, that still bothered him a little. A minute later, the other two officers came into the room.

"Erin O'Malley, I presume," the other detective said.

"Yeah," Bradham replied dejectedly. "One in the chest, one in the head. Just like the others."

"Why would Coulson do it? Doesn't seem like she was much of a threat. At least there's nothing in her package that would indicate so."

"Probably just tying up loose ends. He used her for what he needed her for. A place to stay so he didn't have to use a hotel and be traced, use of a car so he couldn't be tracked with a rental, and having her go into a store and pay for things so he wouldn't be seen on camera. Who knows? Could be all of those reasons and plenty more. Who knows with a psycho like that?"

"I'll call the coroner."

"Get the crime scene unit down here too." Bradham then looked at the uniformed officer. "Start roping off the area."

"Will do."

Bradham started looking around the room, being careful not to touch or disturb anything since he didn't have gloves on. He then went back downstairs and went out the same way they came in. He met the other detective on the back lawn.

"CSU will be here in about ten minutes. Coroner will probably be about twenty."

Bradham nodded.

"What do you think happened in there?"

"Looks like a heck of a struggle to me," Bradham replied.

"I'm thinking yesterday by the looks of the body."

"Yeah, sounds about right."

"The way I'm figuring it, they might have been in this small room there off the kitchen," the detective said, pointing to it. "That's when Coulson makes his move. She somehow gets away or fights him off, running into the living room, where they struggle some more. She's able to get away again, this time running upstairs, not even thinking, just going wherever's available to her. Unfortunately, she closes herself off, Coulson follows her up there, then kills her."

Bradham nodded again. It was the same way he'd sized it up. "We need to get an APB out on that car too. It's not here, so there's a good chance he still has it."

"Might have ditched it by now."

"Maybe. Still need to find it, though."

As the detective went back to his car to get on the radio, Bradham looked at the house for a minute, still seeing images of the dead woman in his mind. It bothered him. The woman never stood a chance with a creep like Coulson. And while he couldn't say for a fact that she wasn't somehow implicated in anything, his gut was telling him no. He believed her to be an innocent victim until he got proof otherwise. He didn't think he'd ever get that proof, though. He supposed it was still good that he got bothered by these types of things sometimes. Some of the other detectives and officers he had met over the years had become hardened to these types of things, seeing them far too often. That was something he never wanted to do. Get used to it. Seeing a dead body shouldn't be considered normal. It should be a sad event, something that affected everyone involved. If he ever got to the point where he didn't feel something, that's when he knew it would be time to retire. Luckily, he wasn't there yet. But finding the man that did it, that was the thing that was going to keep him going. And he wouldn't stop until he got there.

13

A few days had passed, and while the manhunt for Remi Coulson was still on, all the leads had grown cold. Nobody knew where he was or even had an idea if he was still in California. Hall and Charlotte had just gotten back to their apartment after talking to a few people that knew Carly Learson, still trying to get a better grip on what had happened. They sat down at the kitchen table and started talking when Hall's phone rang. It was Bradham.

"Hey, what's up?" Hall said.

"I'm gonna ask a favor of you."

"Sure, what is it?"

"It pains me to even say this, especially since you're not on the force. I shouldn't even be asking this of a civilian."

"What's the problem?"

"Thurmond got kicked loose this morning."

"He's out of jail?"

"Yeah. He buckled up and got a lawyer, recanted everything he said, said he made the statements under duress."

"That's a crock."

"Yeah, but it is what it is," Bradham said. "We don't really have any evidence to corroborate anything he said right now, so the superiors told me to drop the charges for now."

"What about the girlfriend?"

"She got kicked loose a couple days ago. We didn't really have anything that could stick on her either."

"So what do you need me for?"

"Could you keep an eye on him for me?"

"Who? Thurmond?"

"Yeah."

"What for?"

"'Cause he's involved in all this up to his neck," Bradham replied. "And right now, he's the only one still alive who can talk about it. Whoever this Ripper guy is, he has already had Coulson take out the other members of the group."

"And you think he's gonna do it to Thurmond too?"

"I dunno. Unless Thurmond's in really good with this guy and Ripper doesn't think he'll talk, maybe not. But it seems to me like Ripper's trying to tape off all the loose ends. Thurmond's the last one in the group that can lead us to Ripper."

"Coulson could too."

"If we could find him, which we can't. We can find Thurmond, though."

"I don't understand what you need me for," Hall said. "Just put one of your guys on him."

"I can't. I don't have a spare man for the job. We're buried in cases, overloaded in suspects, overworked and undermanned. I tried and got shot down. Superiors won't approve tailing someone like Thurmond unless there's a specific threat, and I can't say that there is. It's just a feeling. The only other way we could get a man on him is if we got specific information that he's planning a crime or planning to meet with someone, and I can't say for sure on that either."

"So that's why you're coming to me."

"That's why I'm coming to you."

"I'm the backup plan."

"Hey, you wanted in, I let you in. If you wanna stay in, I'm giving you the option."

"And I don't ever get the runaround on any future cases?" Hall asked, trying to play his cards right. He was planning on helping out his friend anyway, even if he said no to his request. But it didn't hurt to ask and get something out of it, regardless.

"Deal."

"OK, we'll get right on it."

"Thanks. I appreciate it."

"You know where he's at now?"

"Don't know. I doubt he'll go back to his girlfriend's

apartment again. That's why I want you to run him down."

"All right, we'll find him."

"Brandon, let me know when you do, huh?"

"You got it. Hey, before you go, any luck on Coulson yet?"

"Nah, he's in the wind. He could be anywhere in ten different states by now."

"No hits on that car?"

"He's probably long since dumped it by now."

"Well, maybe when we find Thurmond, we'll find him too."

"That's what I'm thinking, buddy. I'm hoping so. This is one I really wanna wrap up soon."

"Well, I better get started. I'll let you know how it goes."

Hall put his phone down and explained the situation to Charlotte. They sat there thinking of their options for a minute, getting out the list of names they had that they initially talked to when they were trying to find Thurmond.

"I don't know how we're gonna find him again," Charlotte said.

One name stuck out, though. "I do." Hall pointed to the name on the paper.

"Hyde."

"If anyone knows where he's at, it's him."

"Yeah, but will he talk to us again?"

Hall checked his wallet and removed a twenty-dollar bill. "I think so."

"Not again, Brandon. We can't keep giving our money away. We'll be in the poorhouse soon."

"It's the last time. I swear."

Charlotte sighed, and even though it was against her better judgment, she agreed. "Fine. The last time."

Hall put his hands up. "Promise."

They immediately left their apartment and drove back over to Melvin Hyde's place. They knocked on the door for a minute with no response.

"You think he's home?" Charlotte asked.

Hall put his ear up to the door and listened. He could clearly hear voices. "They're home."

They continued knocking on the door, getting louder and louder, until it finally opened. The same elderly woman from before answered.

"Isn't this the same thing that happened the last time?" Hall asked.

"Help yas?"

"Uh, Melvin? We'd like to talk to him."

"You cops?"

"You asked us that the last time we were here."

"Maybe you were lying before."

Hall snickered. "No, we're not cops. Can we see Melvin, please?"

"What do you want with him?"

Hall's shoulders slumped, and he felt like beating

his head against the wall. He really didn't want to go through this song and dance again.

"We're private investigators and we want to talk to him. He talked to us before. Can you please just go get him?"

"I don't know."

Hall closed his eyes and started making a clicking noise with his mouth to prevent himself from losing his temper. Charlotte put her hand on his shoulder to keep him calm.

She then took over the conversation for him. "If you just go tell him the same PIs that were here before have something else for him that he would probably like, we'd really appreciate it."

"Well... OK."

The woman closed the door and went inside to find her grandson. Charlotte looked at her boyfriend and smiled. Hall just shook his head.

"You didn't say anything different than I did. Why does she listen to you instead of me?"

Charlotte had to prevent herself from laughing at him. "Maybe you look more threatening."

"I look threatening now because I'm getting mad at this whole stupid runaround. But I didn't when I first knocked."

"Well, maybe I just look like a nicer person who isn't trying to fool her about something."

"What are you saying, I look like a pathological liar or something?"

Charlotte couldn't keep her laughter in any longer. "No, that's not what I'm saying. It's just that…"

Thankfully for her, she didn't have to finish her sentence, as the door opened up again. Hyde stepped outside, closing the door behind him.

"Do you ever do a different setup than this?" Hall asked.

"What? Nah, it works fine. Why change it?"

"It's kind of annoying."

"Says you. You ain't the one who's gotta be looking over his shoulder constantly."

"Well, who's fault is that?"

"Well, if I didn't…"

Charlotte put her hand on her head, interrupting their little discussion before she got a headache. She wasn't really interested in what they were saying anyway, since it was off-topic. "Boys, boys, can we get down to what we're here for?"

"Oh," Hall said. "Yeah. Sorry."

"What are you guys here for?"

"Thurmond."

Hyde put his hands up to his shoulders and took a step back. "Yo, man, listen, I told you I didn't know for sure where the dude was at. I mean, I didn't give no guarantees. I just told you what I knew. Maybe the guy was there, maybe not. That's the price you give for information in this business. Just because he wasn't there, that don't make it my responsibility. This ain't like the department store or nothing, you know.

There ain't no return policy. You gave me the hundred bucks, I told you what I knew, and that's that. Sorry."

"I thought we gave you eighty."

"I thought it was sixty," Charlotte said.

"Listen, sixty, eighty, a hundred, whatever," Hyde said. "There ain't no refunds."

"We're not asking for refunds," Hall said.

"Though it would be nice," Charlotte said.

"The tip you gave us was good."

"Oh. It was?" Hyde said.

"Yes, he was there at that woman's place... Charlene."

"Oh. Then what are you here jamming me up for?"

"We're not jamming you up."

"You're not? What are you here for then?"

"We just wanted to see if you could give us more information about something."

"Oh," Hyde said, his face looking like a combination of anxiety and relief.

"Thurmond was just released from jail," Charlotte said. "We wanted to know where else he might go."

"How am I supposed to know? What am I... his keeper?"

"Listen, we think he might be in trouble."

"Everyone in this line of work is in trouble. Goes with the territory."

"No, we mean real trouble," Hall said. "We think a guy named Remi Coulson might be looking to kill him.

He's already killed three other people. And we think Thurmond might be next on the list."

"What would he wanna do that for?"

"Because he's the last remaining link to some guy named Ripper."

"Jack Ripper?"

Hall and Charlotte looked at each other. "You know him?"

"I know of him. Never did business with the dude or looked at him in the face before. But I've heard his name thrown around."

"What do you know about him?"

"Just that he's a bad dude, man. He's not a guy you wanna be messing with."

"Why?" Charlotte asked.

"Just the word on the street. Word is that if you screw him over somehow, you will be looking up at a pine box and that's the truth. Ain't no doubt about it."

Hall took a picture of Coulson out of his pocket. "What about this guy? You ever seen him before?"

"Didn't you ask me that the last time you were here?"

"I didn't show you a picture the last time we were here."

"Oh. You didn't?"

"No."

"You sure?"

"Positive." Hall then looked at Charlotte, unsure whether they did or not. "Did we?"

Charlotte shook her head. "We did not."

"That's what I thought. See?"

"Oh," Hyde said, looking at the photo closely. "Maybe just 'cause he looks familiar I thought you did."

"He looks familiar?"

"Yeah. Seems like I might have seen him somewhere before."

"Where?"

"I dunno. Can't say for sure. Seems like a face I've seen, but I can't quite picture where right now. I dunno, maybe I've never seen him. Maybe he's just got one of those faces you think you've seen before."

"Well, this is Remi Coulson," Hall said. "We think this guy's killed four people now. And Thurmond might be next."

"Well, I mean, that's Walt's business. If he's mixed up with this Ripper guy, he's gotta expect stuff like this to go down."

"What, you wouldn't do business with him?"

"Who, Ripper?" Hyde asked. "No way, man. There is not enough money in the world that would make me do that. I don't care how good the money is, how easy the job is, I am not getting in bed with that dude. Metaphorically speaking, that is, not literally, 'cause I don't really swing that way, you know what I'm saying? Not that I got a problem with dudes who do that, you understand? But it's just that I—"

"Melvin," Hall said, interrupting him before he went on even more of a tangent.

"Yeah?"

"Nobody cares."

"Oh, well, anyway... I forgot what we were talking about."

Hall looked at Charlotte, almost forgetting himself. Luckily, she saved him. "Remi Coulson," she said. "Walter Thurmond. Know where they might be?"

"Don't know the Coulson dude. I mean, not by name. Maybe not by face either."

"Well, we know you know Thurmond. Where else would he go? I'm sure you know some other places he'd hang out."

Hyde moved his head around like he was trying to relax, moving his eyes everywhere. "I dunno, man, like, it don't feel right informing on the guy all the time."

"What, do you have a limit?" Hall asked.

"Well, you know, it's just, the guy's never really done me no wrong."

Hall rolled his eyes and took the twenty-dollar bill out of his pocket. He held it in the air for a few seconds, Hyde not taking long to snatch it out of his fingers.

"I dunno, man, this is looking pretty lonely."

"It's all we got today."

"I mean, he's just hanging out here by himself, no friends or nothing."

"It's that or nothing."

"Twenty dollars is a pretty cheap price for quality information, you know."

"Listen," Charlotte said, not wanting to hear the games anymore. "It's twenty dollars. Take it or leave it. If you leave it, we'll be back later with Detective Bradham, and I'm pretty sure he's not paying anything these days."

Hyde's eyes widened, and he leaned his head back. "Damn, girl, someone's a little hot under the collar. You got a little spice to you, don't you? A little sweet and sassy! I kind of dig it."

"Trust me, you don't wanna let her get too spicy," Hall said.

"I dunno, I was—"

"Are you gonna tell us or not?!" Charlotte asked, losing her patience.

"Jeez, man, you need to keep this one on a—"

"On a what?!"

"Uh, nothing. Nothing at all. I was just gonna say you're a strong, independent woman, ma'am."

"Uh huh."

"Can we get back to Thurmond?" Hall asked.

"What about him?"

"We want to know where he's at."

"Oh yeah, well..."

"OK, no more games," Charlotte said. "You either tell us now or I'm calling Bradham. He should be able to get here in twenty minutes."

"Damn, girl..." Hyde said, not finishing his

sentence upon seeing Charlotte's eyes shooting daggers at him. "Uh, yeah..."

"You taking the money or no?"

Hyde looked at the woman eerily, then crumpled the twenty-dollar bill and stuffed it in the pocket of his jeans. "Walt, yeah, I mean, I might know a few spots he could be." Charlotte took out a small notepad and pen and listened intently. "I mean, you could check out the other girls he hangs around with. If he feels things are getting hot, he could be changing up his patterns."

"Names and addresses?"

"I can give you some names, maybe an address or two, but I ain't the phone book. I don't know where everyone lives."

"Give us what you got," Hall said.

Hyde proceeded to give a list of eight women, two of whom he knew the address for. The rest he had no idea.

"These are the only ones you know?" Charlotte asked.

"Ain't that enough?!"

"Just wanna make sure you're being thorough."

"That's all I know."

"How's he have so many women? He's not even that good-looking."

Hyde laughed. "Listen, the women he hangs around with, looks ain't exactly the biggest thing on their mind, you know what I'm saying? Walt's the type of guy who needs to have a lot of jobs going on to support his habits."

"What habits?" Hall asked.

"Drugs, gambling, and women. He loves all of them. And they all cost a fortune. Especially the girls he hangs around with. They like that he spends money on them. That's why they stay with him. And, I mean, it's not like they're exclusive or anything. He fools around, they fool around, he spends money on them, everyone gets what they want, right?"

"And that's what's important," Charlotte sarcastically said.

"Hey, if they're all happy, who are we to say?"

"Any other places?" Hall asked. "Besides these women?"

"Uh, nah, not really." Hyde then hesitated for a few seconds, remembering something. "Well, there was one other place."

"What place?"

"There's this hotel off of Crenshaw. Decent place. He sometimes likes to hang out there."

"Why? What's so special about it?"

"'Cause it's like the one hotel that he actually likes."

"What do you mean?"

"Walt's got this thing about hotels, motels, places like that, he hates them. Thinks they're like the dirtiest places, got bugs, germs, things like that, he just can't stand staying in them. But this hotel on Crenshaw, for whatever reason, I don't know, Walt actually likes staying there. So maybe check it out."

"What's the name of it?"

"I dunno, what do I look like, map of America? It's on Crenshaw and the boulevard. Red building. Three floors. That's it."

"OK. Thanks. We'll be back if we need anything else."

"All right, but if you do, make sure you bring some company with you," Hyde said, holding the twenty up. "'Cause, no offense, but this here ain't cutting it. Not for this quality of information. You need to come more prepared for the situation."

"Would you prefer us to take our business elsewhere?"

"Well, I didn't say that now. I just said to come with friends."

"We'll remember that."

14

Hall and Charlotte spent the better part of two days trying to run down all the names on the list that Hyde had given them. A few of them didn't have any permanent address and moved around a lot, usually staying at some rinky-dink hotel that Thurmond wouldn't be caught dead in. It was just after dinner when they found the last name on the list. After a quick conversation, they knew she hadn't seen Thurmond in a couple of months. Every name on the list was a dead end. None of them had seen Thurmond or knew where he was. Once they got back to the car, they figured out their next move.

"What now?" Charlotte asked.

Hall shook his head, not sure. "I dunno."

"We still have that hotel we can check out."

Hall sighed, knowing the chances they'd find Thurmond there were slim and none. "Yeah."

"Let's just go there and see if he's been there. If not, then we'll go home, get a good night's sleep, and figure out what to do next tomorrow."

Hall nodded, thinking it sounded as good as anything. They drove to the hotel, which was about twenty minutes away from the last woman that they'd spoken to. They went in and asked the desk clerk if Walter Thurmond had checked in, but the man said they didn't have anyone currently in the hotel by that name. They gave him a general description, but that didn't seem to ring any bells either. Dejected, they went back to the car.

"We'll find him," Charlotte said, sensing that her boyfriend was getting frustrated.

"Sooner rather than later would be nice."

"Can't rush these things. You know that. It'll happen."

"Hopefully before someone else winds up dead."

Hall glumly looked out the window as the two of them sat silently in the car for a minute. He looked around at all the cars that were surrounding them. The hotel wasn't at full capacity, but there were probably a few dozen cars sitting in the parking lot. Hall's eyes perked up as he looked at one of them. It was familiar for some reason.

"Don't we have the type of car that Thurmond drives?"

"Uh, yeah, I think so," Charlotte said, going through her notebook. "Why?"

Hall pointed to a car in the far corner of the lot, over on her side. "That car down there seems familiar."

"Here it is." Charlotte started reading it off. "It's a 2015 Toyota. Black."

"Isn't that it?" Hall asked, a mix of hope and excitement in his voice.

Charlotte gazed at it for a few seconds. "Can't see the license plate from here, but it sure fits the description."

"Let's go take a look."

The pair got out of the car and went over to the black Toyota, standing just beyond the back bumper as they got a good look at the plate. They looked at the plate, then down at Charlotte's notebook, then back at the plate again to make sure they were reading it correctly.

"That's it," Charlotte said. "It's his car."

"And the guy said he wasn't here."

"Maybe he doesn't think he is. Thurmond might've checked in under a different name. And the clerk might not have been here when he did check in."

"Yeah."

"Well, at least we know he's here. Now comes the hard part. Finding which room he's in."

"Let's head back to the car and wait," Hall said. "See if he comes out anytime soon."

They went back to the car, setting themselves up for possibly a long night. They sat there for over four hours, without a sign of Thurmond anywhere, except for his car.

"You know, this might be pointless," Charlotte said. "I mean, he might not come out until tomorrow. What are we gonna do, just sit here all night?"

"What else can we do? We can't go around knocking on doors. It's almost midnight. That's a good way to get shot."

"It just feels like a waste of time sitting here all night."

"If you want, I can drop you off at home, then come back. Then at least one of us will get some rest."

"No, I'm not leaving you here by yourself."

"Well, I figure we got three options."

"Can't wait to hear them."

"We can continue to sit here and wait."

"Don't like that one," Charlotte said.

"We can go in there again and have another crack at that clerk."

"Maybe."

"Or we can call Bradham and have him come over," Hall said. "Let him deal with finding out where Thurmond is. Then we can all go home sooner."

"I like that one."

"Let's take another shot at the clerk first."

Charlotte puffed. "Why? Let's just call Bradham and get it over with."

"He's busy. I don't wanna call him unless we have to."

"But it's his case!"

Hall got out of the car. "Let's just do it this way first."

Charlotte reluctantly got out of the car and followed her boyfriend back inside the hotel. The clerk was sitting there reading a magazine.

"You guys again?"

"Uh, yeah, we found our friend's car," Hall said. "It's sitting right out there. It's a 2015 black Toyota."

"I'll tell you the same thing I told you before. The guy you're looking for isn't here."

"But his car is right there!"

The clerk shrugged. "Don't mean nothing to me. Maybe he parked here and walked somewhere else?"

"Didn't think of that," Charlotte said, mumbling so low that neither of them heard her.

"I know he's here," Hall said.

"I'll keep saying the same thing, man. He's not here."

"Can you just check the license plate of the car against your records?"

"He's not here."

"You're not even checking."

"'Cause he's not here."

"But you didn't look."

"Don't have to."

Charlotte grabbed her boyfriend by the arm and started pulling on him. "C'mon, Brandon, let's just go."

"He's lying."

"Yeah, probably, let's just go anyway."

Hall reluctantly let himself be pulled away, Charlotte putting her arm around him as they walked out of the office.

"He's lying," Hall said.

"Yeah, probably."

"So why'd you pull me away so fast?"

"Because he's not gonna tell us anything. I think he made that clear."

"Maybe I should—"

"No, we're gonna go back to the car, call Bradham, and let him deal with it."

Hall sighed, but agreed. They got in the car, Hall trying to calm himself down. Charlotte pulled out her phone.

"You know I'm right, right?" she said.

Hall nodded, though he didn't like admitting it. "Yeah." He continued shaking his head for a few more seconds, the clerk still annoying him.

"Relax, don't let it get to you. You know it's part of the deal."

"I just hate getting lied to. Right to my face." Hall kept shaking his head, causing Charlotte to put her hand on the side of his head. She called Bradham, keeping her hand on her boyfriend's head to prevent him from shaking it anymore.

As soon as Bradham picked up, he assumed something was wrong. "What's the matter?"

"Nothing," Charlotte replied.

Dark Day

"Then why are you calling so late? Brandon get beat up again?"

"No, he did not get beat up again."

"I never got beat up in the first place," Hall said, slamming his hands on the steering wheel. "I'm never gonna live that down."

"That's a matter of opinion," Bradham said loudly, hoping his friend could hear him, even though he couldn't.

Charlotte tilted her head and pulled the phone away from her ear until the detective's voice returned to normal. "Anyway, I'm calling because of Walt Thurmond."

"What about him?"

"We've found him."

"You're kidding."

"Would I kid you about that?"

"I didn't mean seriously," Bradham said. "You really found him?"

"We found his car outside a hotel. We've been sitting on it for a few hours, waiting for him to come out, but he hasn't showed yet. We talked to the desk clerk inside who insists that he's never seen or heard of Thurmond, even though we got a tip that this is like the only hotel that Thurmond likes to go to."

"Where'd you get that tip?"

"Can't say."

"Oh, another one of those?"

"So we're sitting outside this hotel, his car in sight,

but we don't know if he's inside. We assume he is, but we don't know a room number."

"So what do you want me to do? Come down and get all badge-heavy?"

"I don't know. Whatever it is you guys do to get the information you want."

"This ain't 1920 anymore. We can't beat it out of him."

"Can't you get a warrant or something?"

"Probably will take a couple hours."

"I mean, we can keep on sitting here for a while, but we assumed there might be a faster way if you got involved."

Bradham made a few noises with his mouth as he thought. "Yeah, sit tight for a bit. I'll be down there soon and see if I can persuade the clerk to cooperate."

"OK."

"Text me the address and I'll leave now."

Charlotte immediately texted the detective the name and address of the hotel, then told Hall he was coming.

"What's he gonna do?" Hall asked.

"I don't know. He didn't say. Just said he'd see if he could persuade the clerk to talk, I guess."

"Persuade? What's he gonna do, charm him into talking?"

"He didn't exactly say."

"I mean, Bradham's a good guy and all, but charm isn't high on his list of attributes."

Charlotte shrugged. "Like I said, he didn't say."

"He's not getting a warrant?"

"Didn't sound like it."

"Hmm. Wonder what he's planning."

"I don't know. He did say they couldn't beat it out of him like they did in the old days."

"So he just wants us to wait?"

"That's what he said."

"For how long?" Hall asked.

"Until he gets here. Said he'd be leaving soon, so I would think he'd be here within half an hour. Probably sooner."

Their wait lasted about twenty-five minutes. Bradham recognized Charlotte's car and pulled up right alongside them. He got out and walked toward them. They had also gotten out of their car by now. The three of them stood by the front of the bumper.

"Didn't bring backup?" Hall asked.

"They're coming," Bradham replied. "Still no sign of Thurmond?"

"Haven't seen anyone come in or out in the last two hours."

"OK." Bradham looked around, waiting to see when the patrol cars were getting there. Two were supposed to be on the way. One then came in the entrance, followed by another one only a few seconds later.

"So what's the plan?" Charlotte asked.

"The plan is I'm gonna go ask the clerk nicely to cooperate."

"That's a waste of time," Hall said. "We've already done that."

Bradham smiled. "Yeah. You may be tough and all, but you can't do the things I can do."

"What's that mean?"

"You'll see."

The other officers then approached the group, with Bradham giving them direction as to what he wanted.

"You stay out here," Bradham said, pointing to one. "If Thurmond makes a break for it and comes this way, he's yours."

The officer nodded. "Got it."

Bradham then looked to the other officer. "There's a back entrance to this building. Go find it and wait there. If he splits out the back, you've got him."

"I'm on it."

"I didn't know there was a back way," Hall said.

"The benefits of being here on another case," Bradham replied.

"What case was that?" Charlotte asked.

"Narcotics bust a year or two ago. Guy actually tried to slip out the back. Luckily, we had the place covered, and we got him, anyway."

Before going in to talk to the clerk, Bradham waited until his officer radioed in that he had the back covered. Just in case Thurmond had a system in place where he got notified if someone was asking about him, Bradham made sure he had all the exits covered.

"You know, it's possible this guy split a long time ago," Bradham said.

"Through the back?" Hall asked, kicking himself for not checking whether there was a back entrance.

"Yeah. If this guy is here from time to time, and the clerks know him and are friendly with him, Thurmond might give them a few extra bucks to let him know if someone's asking about him."

"So once we went in there asking, the clerk phones him up and says someone's looking for you, then he splits out the back," Charlotte said.

"Wouldn't be the first time. Happens quite a bit to be honest."

"So we've been sitting here for nothing," Hall said, already assuming it was a lost cause.

"Not necessarily," Bradham said. "This clerk might know more about Thurmond, places he goes, people he sees, people that might come here specifically. All might not be lost. Not yet, at least."

Once Bradham got the notification that the officer was in place, the three of them went back inside the office. The clerk saw the two familiar faces and sighed, not wanting to go through the whole song and dance again.

"Listen, it's the same answer I gave you guys the other times. I don't know the guy."

Bradham took out his badge and showed it to him. "You wanna change your story?"

The clerk tilted his head and looked away, taking a deep breath, knowing he was about to get jammed up. "What do you want from me?"

"How 'bout the truth for starters?" Hall replied.

Bradham put his hand on Hall's chest to have him calm down. "Walter Thurmond. I know he's here; his car's out there."

"Like I've been telling these people. That don't mean he's here. He could've walked anywhere."

"You really want me to knock on every single one of the doors in this place until I find him?"

"You can't do that. You got a warrant?"

"I don't need a warrant to knock. I'm not searching. But I can knock on every door in this place and show them a picture of Thurmond to see if anyone has seen him around."

"You can't do that. Some of these people are sleeping."

"I was here a couple years ago on a drug bust. I know what some of the people are doing. And sleeping ain't on the list."

"C'mon, man, what do you wanna go rousting me for?"

"I'm not rousting you," Bradham answered. "Just want you to tell me what you know. The sooner you do that, the sooner I'll be out of your hair."

"OK, maybe I've seen the guy from time to time, but he's not here now."

"Then where is he?"

"Search me. He doesn't give me his itinerary, you know."

"Why's his car out there?"

The clerk shrugged. "Again, search me."

"Is that a consent from you?"

"It's a figure of speech, man."

"OK, well, listen, we can make this as easy or as hard as you wanna make it," Bradham said.

"I just want you guys to get out of here and stop pestering me."

"We'll stop pestering you when you actually tell us the truth. I've been in this game a long time. And I can tell when someone's lying to me. And I can tell right now that you know more than you're saying. You've got that guilty, lying look about you."

"You're crazy."

Bradham looked closer at the man's name tag. "Listen, Herb. How much business you want up in this joint over the next few days?"

"What's that supposed to mean?"

"Well, if you wanna look out this window here, you'll see two patrol cars sitting by the front entrance. Now, I'm not some expert marketer or anything, but I'm assuming that having two patrol cars just sit here for a few days while we wait for Thurmond, I kind of assume that's bad for business. I mean, who's gonna wanna come in here for a room with cops all over the place? They're gonna assume that something's wrong."

"You can't do that. That's… I dunno… something. You can't do that."

"Oh, I can. I mean, we're allowed to park. We're not blocking an entrance, we're not preventing anyone from coming in, we're not trying to catch anyone or trap anyone, we're just sitting there writing reports. We can do that, you know."

The clerk took a gulp. "You can't just have cops sitting there all day."

"They'll be sitting there. All day, all night, for the next few days, until we find what we want to find. Now, we can speed things up a bit if you want to just cooperate."

Herb wiped the sweat off his forehead. "You guys sure play dirty sometimes."

"It becomes necessary when dealing with the likes of you guys. So what's it gonna be?" Bradham asked. "Are you gonna tell us what we want to know? Or do we have to sit here for a few days and ruin your business? 'Cause something tells me, if we're sitting out there for three days, it's gonna be like a ghost town in here."

The clerk slumped his shoulders, knowing he was licked. He then started nodding, giving up. "Yeah, yeah."

"So he's here?"

Herb continued nodding. "Room 203. Up the stairs to the left."

"So how's it usually work?" Bradham asked. "He gives you money if you cover for him?"

Herb nodded one more time. "If someone asks about him, I'm supposed to say he's not here. Then when the person leaves, I call Walt, and he gives me ten bucks."

"Nice system you got going on there."

Herb shrugged. "Works for him."

Bradham then slapped his hand on the counter. "Stay off that phone. I hear a phone ringing in his room, I'm gonna come back down here and arrest you as an accessory."

Herb put his hands up. "I'm off, I'm off. It's his problem now."

"Don't go anywhere either. I'll wanna talk to you when we get back."

Herb sighed and nodded, knowing he was up against it now. Hall, Charlotte, and Bradham left the office, finding the outside stairs that led up to the second floor.

"Everyone's in position," Bradham said. "Let's do this."

15

Before going up the steps to Thurmond's room, Bradham looked at his two friends by his side. He was OK with Hall going up with him, making sure he had some backup with not having any other police personnel available to be with him. But without knowing what they were walking into, he wanted to make sure Charlotte was safe.

"You wait here," Bradham said, looking at Charlotte.

She shook her head, not liking that direction. "Nope."

"What do you mean, no? You can't go up there."

"Why not?"

"You're not a trained professional."

"Well, he's not either," Charlotte said, pointing to her boyfriend.

"Well, he was in the military, plus he's a licensed PI,

plus he's licensed to carry a gun. You are and have none of those things."

"I go where he goes."

"Charlotte."

"No. I'm going where he goes. That simple."

Bradham looked at Hall, not believing how stubborn his girlfriend was being. "Would you talk to her?"

"I'd like to, but it wouldn't do any good," Hall answered. "That's her rule. Right behind me. Always."

"You can't tell her to stay behind?"

"I could. But she won't."

Bradham looked up to the black sky. "And up until now, I thought you were the stubborn one. What happened to nice, innocent, angelic looking Charlotte?"

"Oh, she went to bed," Charlotte replied with a smile. "She told me to come in her place."

"Unbelievable."

Bradham started walking up the steps, followed by Hall. And Charlotte. Bradham stopped about halfway up, then looked back at the woman who was still following them. Charlotte gave him a sweet-looking smile and waved at him. Bradham shook his head and kept going. Once they got to the top of the steps, Bradham looked to Charlotte again.

"OK, you're up here," Bradham said. "But you're going to stay here until we tell you it's safe to come down." They were only three doors away from Thurmond's, but the detective was not going to take chances with her life if Thurmond decided he didn't want to talk or cooperate anymore.

"But..."

"No buts. You will stay here until we check it out first. You'll either do that, or I'll put you in handcuffs and put you in a patrol car until this is over."

Charlotte looked to her boyfriend. "Are you just gonna let him do that?"

"Yes, he is!"

Hall shrugged. "I don't think I have very much say in this debate."

"Which one do you prefer?" Bradham asked. "Here or the car?"

Charlotte sighed. "Fine. I'll stay here. But I'm coming in after you open that door."

"We'll wave to you when it's safe."

"I'm not a delicate flower, you know."

"Just... wait. OK?"

Charlotte gave sort of a nod, making a displeased face along with it. "Fine."

Hall and Bradham walked across the platform until they got to room 203. There didn't appear to be any lights on inside. Bradham put his head to the door to listen for sounds, but there was nothing. Not even a TV or a radio. He looked at Hall and shook his head. Bradham stood to the side of the door, which was usually the procedure when a cop wasn't sure what awaited him on the other side of it. There had been instances where an officer was shot through a door after knocking. Bradham waved at Hall to get behind him. The detective knocked several times. After waiting a few seconds, Bradham knocked again. After getting no answer, Bradham tried to listen at the door again, figuring he would at least hear someone getting up to check who was at the door. It was silent as could be, though.

"Maybe the clerk was right," Hall said. "Maybe he did take a walk."

"Most people don't take walks around the neighborhood at midnight."

"Maybe he's robbing some place as he does it." Bradham didn't find the joke humorous and kept knocking, this time even louder. "Maybe he's a heavy sleeper."

"Well, it's time he woke up then," Bradham said, knocking so hard he could have woken up an elephant. After another minute of knocking, he was starting to lose his patience. "C'mon, Thurmond, we know you're in there! Open up!"

Still getting no answer, Bradham went over to the window and started tapping on the glass. He kept tapping on it, harder and harder. He sighed, frustrated they weren't getting a response.

"This is ridiculous. I know he's in there."

"Can't you just break the door down?" Hall asked.

"No, I can't just break the door down. Not without a valid reason."

Charlotte was tired of waiting in her designated

spot, so she went down to see her friends. "I see you're not having much luck."

"How'd you get here?" Bradham asked. "I told you to wait down there."

"Well, I just walked, and there doesn't seem to be much of a threat since you can't even get the door open."

Bradham couldn't really argue that point. The three of them then stood around for the next few minutes, discussing their options.

"Doesn't the manager or the clerk have a key for all the rooms?" Hall asked.

"Yeah, should," Bradham replied.

"Can't we just get him to open the door?"

"Can he do that?" Charlotte asked. "Legally, I mean."

"Well, hotel staff does have the right to open any door if they think there's a problem or an issue inside," the detective said.

"Are you allowed to kind of push him in that direction?" Hall asked.

"That's a slippery legal slope. If it got to court, I have a feeling anything we found in there would probably be thrown out since there's been no complaints, and we don't hear anything wrong. But considering we just wanna talk to him, and we're not looking to arrest him, it should probably be all right. I mean, we're just checking on his well-being, right?"

"Right."

"Then I don't see the harm in asking the hotel if they could open the door so we can make sure Thurmond is all right."

"I'm with ya," Hall said.

"OK, you go down there and tell him to come up with a key to the room."

"Why me? Am I allowed to do that?"

"Just tell him I sent you down there and want him up here with a key."

"So why don't you do it?"

"Because I'm the only police officer up here, and I gotta stay by the door in case he opens it."

"I can do that."

"No, you can't," Bradham said. "Do you wanna go get the clerk or not?"

"I guess so."

Hall left the others and went back down the stairs to the main office. The clerk was still standing there, reading his magazine like nothing else was going on.

"Yes?" Herb asked, knowing there was something else they wanted.

"Detective Bradham wants you up there with a key."

"What for?"

"He wants you to unlock the room," Hall answered.

"Why?"

"Well, as far as I understand it, it's either you open the door for him, or he's gonna knock it down. I assume you'd rather do it the easy way so you don't have to worry about fixing a door?"

"Hey, if he breaks a door, he's gonna pay for it."

Hall nodded, not really interested in what he had to say. "Yeah, yeah, just get up there with a key."

"Fine."

Herb grabbed the master set of keys and started going up the steps, sorting the keys out until he found the one for 203. Hall was right behind him, making sure he didn't make a run for it or anything. It wouldn't have surprised Hall if he did. He didn't trust him for anything. Once the pair got up to the second floor, they immediately went over to Bradham, who was standing just beyond the window, still making sure he wasn't a target in case someone decided to blast the windows out.

"What do you wanna open the door for?" Herb asked.

"Because I wanna do a healthcare check and make sure the man isn't hurt or injured," Bradham replied.

"A healthcare check, huh? Doesn't sound legal to me."

"It's right there in the rule book. Section 106, subsection 52, article 76, paragraph 31. Police have a right to open any door if they believe the occupant inside the room of whatever door they're going in may be hurt, injured, or unable to defend or take care of themselves."

"Oh."

As Herb went over to the door and stuck the key in to unlock it, Bradham looked at Hall and Charlotte, a small grin on his face. He shrugged and tilted his head to the side, thinking everything he said sounded good. Nothing he'd just said was actually in the rule book, at least not as far as he knew. Well, maybe it was in there, but he wasn't one of those cops who could recite it chapter and verse. He knew of a few cops who could do that, but Bradham just never had the time for all that. He was too busy chasing down the bad guys. And while he generally knew the law and what he could or couldn't do, if there was any doubt in his mind, he generally erred on the side of caution and got clarification first or stepped aside. This wasn't one of those times.

"Just unlock the door and then step back," Bradham said.

Herb did as he was ordered and took a few steps back out of the way. Bradham took his gun out. He then looked at Hall to do the same since he was backing him up.

"You gonna get your gun out?"

"I don't have it," Hall answered.

"What? Where is it?"

"It's in the car."

"What's it doing there?"

"I didn't know I'd need it. You didn't tell me to bring it."

"Don't you carry it with you? You're licensed."

"I don't really like carrying it."

"He feels he doesn't really need one," Charlotte said. "He feels he can usually take care of any situation with his hands and feet."

Bradham rolled his eyes. "Yeah, I know you're good with all that kung fu stuff, but sometimes it's good to go a little further and take that extra step."

Hall shrugged. "Sorry."

"All that mumbo jumbo nonsense didn't help you much with Coulson did it?"

Hall looked up at the sky. "Oh my god, are we ever gonna get off that? He caught me with one shot."

"Uh huh."

"You want me to go down and get my gun?"

"No, we'll just go in like this," Bradham replied. "Stay sharp."

Bradham went over to the door and slowly turned the handle, not that he was sure why. Thurmond obviously knew they were there by now. They weren't sneaking up on anybody. Bradham pushed the door open, crouching down in case a bullet was fired where his head would have been. Bradham rushed inside, clinging to the wall as he felt around for the light switch. He finally found it a few seconds later, flipping it on.

"Brandon."

Bradham put his gun away, looking at the floor of the room, knowing there would be no need for his gun. Not anymore. Hall walked in, wondering why the

Dark Day

detective sounded so calm. He didn't have to wonder long, though. There it was, lying right in the middle of the floor. Thurmond's body. He was on his back.

"What's going on in there?" Charlotte asked, walking into the room herself.

Herb also followed her in. They both saw the issue immediately as well.

"Charlotte," Bradham said. "Go get those other two officers and tell them to come up here."

"OK."

Charlotte immediately went and got the other officers, who instantly went up to the second-floor room to get further instructions from the detective. Bradham, Hall, and the clerk stepped out of the room and closed the door to prevent anyone from tampering with the crime scene.

"You stay here on the door," Bradham told the one officer. "Nobody in except for the usual people."

"Right."

Bradham then turned to the other officer. "Go call it in. Get everyone and their mother down here."

"Will do."

"You want us to stay?" Hall asked.

"Just for a little while. There'll be a few other detectives coming down. Just want you to talk to them, corroborate everything I say about what happened here."

Hall nodded, feeling a little sad about what happened in that room. Thurmond certainly was no angel, but he didn't deserve to be murdered. Nobody did. And not executed like that either.

"How long does it look like he's been dead for?" Charlotte asked.

"Oh, I'd say maybe... twenty-four hours?" Bradham replied. "Something like that. Medical examiner will have a better idea and can narrow it down further, but I'd say something like that. Twenty-four, thirty-six, somewhere in that range."

"Good thing we caught this when we did. Otherwise, who knows how long it would have taken to find him."

"Well, it probably wouldn't have been too long. The cleaning crew would have had to come in at some point, and they would have found him. So it's likely we would have found him in the next day or two anyway. But, finding a body earlier rather than later is always a good thing. It's always tougher when more time has passed."

"It's too bad we didn't get here sooner. Then we might have been able to see whoever did it running out of there."

"Yeah. But I don't think we need to see a face to know who it was," Bradham said. "Did you notice the pattern?"

Hall nodded. "Same as the others. One in the chest, one in the head."

"Coulson beat us here."

"How?"

Bradham shrugged. "He must've gotten good information somewhere. Maybe the same place you did."

"No, I don't think so. Though I couldn't say definitely."

"Well, in any case, I think that might be the last of the bodies for a while."

"What makes you think that?"

"That's the last of the loose ends. At least as far as we know. There's nobody left in the scheme to kill, unless there's more players that we don't know about yet."

"There's always Coulson."

"Yeah, a guy we can't find," Bradham said. "And I don't think he'd be on the hit list."

"Why not?"

"Because you usually don't kill guys who can kill as efficiently as he can. Plus, guys like him generally don't talk. There's no benefit for them to do so. They've already got life in prison, there's no deal that's gonna get them out of that. Instead of a hundred and fifty years, they get a hundred? Still a death sentence either way. And guys like Coulson generally don't get taken alive. They prefer to go out on their shield."

"It all comes down to Ripper than."

Bradham nodded, knowing that would be hard, if not impossible. "That's what it's looking like."

"Unless we can somehow get Coulson and convince him to tell us what he knows."

"I think you're pipe dreaming there."

16

It'd been two days since Thurmond's body had been found. The police had no leads. Though from the way the body was positioned, and the same wounds as the other victims, there was no doubt in Bradham's mind who was responsible. But he couldn't prove it yet. Not until he got a ballistics report back from the crime lab. And even that wouldn't be specific proof. Just one more thing to put in the belt. They had no witnesses. Nobody saw anyone go into or come out of Thurmond's room in the previous two days from when the body was found. And nobody heard a thing, though that wasn't necessarily a surprise to Bradham. It was likely that Coulson had used a silencer or a suppressor. It was just as likely that anyone in that building might have seen or heard something, but just didn't want to get involved. That hotel was known for people staying

Dark Day

who were on the wrong side of the tracks. And most of them didn't like talking to the police, even if they weren't the subject of an investigation.

Hall and Charlotte were doing their part in trying to help, talking to everyone they could. Bradham didn't mind them helping out in this case. He knew that sometimes people just wouldn't open up to the police, no matter how hard they tried. But they might decide to talk to someone who wasn't an official law enforcement officer. Someone like a private investigator. Unfortunately, they came up with dead ends too. Nobody admitted to Hall and Charlotte anything different from what they told the police. Everyone was deaf and dumb.

Hall and Charlotte had been driving around town aimlessly for the last several minutes, ever since they'd interviewed the last person on their list, a woman who had been staying at the hotel the same time as Thurmond. They figured there was more they could do, they just weren't sure what. Eventually, Hall got tired of driving to nowhere, and thought of something. He didn't know if it would lead anywhere, but it was something. It might have been a slim chance, but a slim chance was better than no chance.

"Hyde."

"What?" Charlotte asked.

"Hyde. Maybe he knows something."

"Oh, no, not again."

"You've gotta admit, the man seems to know what's going on."

"Yeah, but he can't know everything."

"Well, let's find out."

"Brandon, no, we don't have any more money."

"I've got ten dollars."

Charlotte's shoulders slumped, and she hung her head. "This guy's gonna make us go broke, I swear."

"We'll be fine. It's just ten dollars."

"On top of twenty dollars on top of eighty dollars, on top of, on top of, on top of."

"I thought it was sixty dollars?"

"Whatever. You get my point."

"We can afford ten dollars. Just means we don't go out for coffee this week."

"We don't go out for coffee, anyway."

"You know what I'm saying," Hall said.

"Unfortunately, I do. It means you're saying we're giving our money away."

"Hey, if he can actually tell us something useful, it's not being thrown away."

"In your opinion."

"This is the last time, I promise."

"I think you said that the last time."

"I did? Well, this'll be it."

"I doubt it."

They drove to the Hyde residence, knocking on the door, and just like the other times, the same woman answered. And she asked the same questions like she had never seen them before.

"You think he ever answers the door?" Charlotte asked.

"If you were in his line of work, would you?"

"Good point. You'd think they would switch it up every now and then, though. Maybe have a different family member cross-examine us."

"Why fix something that seems to work?"

Hyde came to the door fairly quickly this time. Since Hall and Charlotte seemed to be regular visitors, they were beginning to earn more trust. That meant their wait time was being cut down. They were already vetted and deemed OK.

"You guys again?" Hyde asked upon seeing them. "Man, you guys are gonna hurt my image being here so often."

"Believe me, it pained me too," Charlotte said.

Hyde smiled. "Yeah, I bet. So what do you guys need now?"

"Walter Thurmond is dead," Hall replied.

"Yeah, I heard about it yesterday. Too bad. Walt seemed like an all-right guy."

Hall took out the photo of Coulson again and showed it to him. "This is the guy we think did it. Remi Coulson."

"Yeah, that's the dude you showed me the last time you were here."

"Anything get jogged loose? Remember him now?"

Hyde shook his head. "Nah, still don't ring any bells."

"Last time you thought you might've seen him."

"Yo, I might have seen a lot of guys, that don't mean I remember them or where I saw them. Could've been a strip joint for all I know."

"Pleasant memories," Charlotte said sarcastically.

"You ain't kidding there," Hyde said, his face lighting up like he remembered one of the ladies.

"You gotta know something about this guy," Hall said. "You're connected in this town. You know everybody. Where would this guy go, hang out?"

"I don't know. You got me on that one." Hall looked at him like he didn't believe him. "Seriously, man, I don't know."

"OK, what about Ripper?"

"Man, you don't wanna be messing with him."

"That's not what I asked. Where's he hang out, where do people go to meet him, things like that?"

"First of all, from what I understand, Ripper chooses you. There's no meeting or whatever. If he picks you, he finds you, then you accept his deal or not."

"He must live and hangout somewhere," Hall said. "He must go somewhere that's familiar to him. Right?"

"Uh, yeah, man, I guess."

"So where would that be?" Hyde started looking around outside. "You doing this again?"

"Man, when you're talking about Ripper, anytime

you mention that dude, it means he knows you're onto him too probably, which means he might be out there watching right now. Which puts a bullseye on my back too."

"Then help us out by telling us where we can find him."

Hyde scratched his face along his jaw, clearly thinking about whether he should reveal anything. It was obvious he knew something he wasn't telling yet. Hall removed the money from his wallet and held it in the air. Hyde immediately took it, not liking money being flashed in the air for too long. If anybody was watching, it would be a sure sign of a payoff. Hyde held the money in his hand and looked at it. He turned the bill over a few times, thinking a couple of the bills must have been stuck together. Once he realized it was only one bill, he scowled.

"Ten dollars?! Are you kidding me? Ten dollars?"

"It's all we got," Hall answered.

"Ten lousy stinking dollars?! You can't pony up more than that?"

"Told you, it's all we got."

"You're talking about one of the biggest fish in this city, and that's all you can come up with?"

"You're free to say no," Charlotte said.

"Yeah, you'd like that, wouldn't you?"

"Actually, I would. I'd rather have my ten dollars back."

Hyde stuck the money in his pocket.

"Uh, that money was for information," Hall said. "It wasn't a down payment or something."

"Well, when you come back with the rest of the money, I might tell you something."

"Melvin, you really don't wanna do that?"

"Do what?"

"Stiff me."

"Why not? Whatcha gonna do about it?"

Charlotte closed her eyes and shook her head. Hyde noticed what she was doing and wondered what was wrong with her.

"You really don't wanna do that?" Charlotte said, opening her eyes.

"Do what?"

"You don't wanna make him mad."

"Why?" Hyde looked Hall over. "He some type of badass or something?"

"I was in the military as an MP, also in special forces, and I also know and am proficient in six different forms of martial arts." Hall stood there, a confident look on his face. He was sure Hyde didn't want to mess with him. Not now. "Why would you wanna mess things up now? We've been getting the information we want, you've been making money, everyone's been happy. You don't wanna ruin that now."

Hyde continued looking Hall over. He had that ex-military vibe to him, and he looked like he was still in good shape. He didn't really have much doubt about any of Hall's claims.

"So you're either gonna tell us what you know," Hall said, "or you're going to give me that money back. Right now. There's no in between."

"Can't you just come back in a week or something with another fifty or something?" Hyde asked.

"We don't have a week to wait. By that time Ripper and Coulson will probably be gone. The trail's hot now. We need to find them now. You either take the ten and spill what you know, or we'll find out who your competition is and see if they wanna start making some extra money from us."

"Awe, that ain't right, man. Going to other people instead of me."

"It's up to you."

"It just ain't right. I mean, after all the tips I've given you already that have panned out. And you're gonna do me like that by going to my competition?"

"It's a rough world out there."

"Yeah, you ain't gotta tell me."

"Time's a wasting," Charlotte said. "No more chit chat. You either want the money or you don't. Let's go."

Hyde looked at her, then Hall. "Man, she really don't like being here, does she? I can tell."

"Not really," Hall said.

"It shows."

"An answer?" Charlotte asked.

"All right, all right, keep your pants on." Hyde then checked her out a little more. "Though in your case..." He started smiling, thinking about what she might look like under her clothes. Then he caught himself and looked back at Hall, not wanting to anger him in case they were together. "Uh, wait a minute, are you two, like... a thing?"

"A thing?" Hall asked.

"Yeah, you know, like, together? Co-mingling?"

"Yeah, we're a thing."

"Oh," Hyde said, the smile instantly wiped from his face. "Sorry, man, I wasn't trying to, like, you know." Hyde gestured to Charlotte, though his hands were pretty much going all over the place. "I didn't know you guys were, I mean, I wasn't trying to, well..."

Hall wasn't interested in any of that. He just wanted to speed the process along. "Yeah, yeah, it's fine. I don't care. Are you gonna tell us about Ripper or not? We need to get moving."

"Uh, yeah, Ripper. Rumor has it that he likes to do business in some worn-out building on Kings Street."

"What building?"

"I don't know the number or anything. I just know the place used to be some type of dry-cleaning store."

"Ever been there?" Hall asked.

"I mean, I drove by it a few times, but I never stepped inside or nothing. You don't go into those places unless you're invited. And if you ain't invited, and you go in there, believe me, you won't live long enough to actually be invited."

"That it?"

"Well, rumor also has it that there might be a girl who knows him. Works at the Hot Stuff strip club."

"The Hot Stuff strip club?" Charlotte asked.

"Yeah, ever been there?"

"No!"

"Shame, man, you might, um, fit in," Hyde said with a smile.

"I wouldn't be caught dead working in a place like that."

"That's what half them girls said too before they started working there."

"Can we get back on topic?" Hall asked. "What's this girl's name?"

"Candy."

"Candy?"

"Yeah, 'cause she's as sweet as…"

"Yeah, I get the point."

"What kind of name is Candy?" Charlotte asked. "I mean, that's so… typical."

"Listen," Hyde said. "When you work in one of them joints, you gotta stand out. I mean, besides the usual ways you would stand out if you know what I mean. One of those ways is with a catchy name that fits the environment that you're working in."

"So she's a dancer?" Hall asked.

"Uh, yeah, I guess you could call it that. It's not really one of those high-class joints where you take your time and enjoy yourself."

"Who would enjoy themselves?" Charlotte asked.

Hyde snickered. "Man, you gotta take her out more. Anyway, it's one of those places where you get on stage, make a few moves, show everyone what you got, then get off stage."

"Is she one of the more popular attractions there?" Hall asked.

Hall moved his head around, thinking. "Yeah, I guess you could say that."

"What's she look like?"

Hyde smiled, wondering how he could phrase it best. He then looked at Charlotte. "You wanna cover your ears or something?"

Charlotte gave him an unpleasant face. "I think I can handle it."

"Suit yourself. But man, she is fine. Pretty face, though who's really looking, know what I'm saying?" Hyde laughed. "But anyway, real nice legs, tan, thin, but not stick thin or nothing, just real solid. Ass is, mmm, sweet, firm. Nice abs, toned, real sweet looking. Boobs, big, man. You could put your head on them oversized pillows and feel like you're on cloud nine or something. You could fall asleep on those puppies."

"Wow. You have totally just objectified her."

"Say what?"

"I mean, you talk about her like she's not even a person. She's just a thing for you to drool over."

"So?"

Hall could see his girlfriend was getting agitated, so

he put his hand on her arm to calm her down. "Don't even bother. He's not gonna understand."

"Understand what?" Hyde asked.

"Never mind. All I asked was what she looked like."

"And I told you!"

"You described everything about her except her face. You know, what people really look like."

"Who's got time to notice that?"

"Well, you noticed everything else about her apparently," Charlotte said.

Hyde laughed. "'Cause there's so much else of her to notice."

Charlotte shook her head. "You're such a pig."

"Hey, I'm not the one who's making her go up there and take her clothes off. She's doing that all on her own. If you're doing that all by yourself, then you want people to be looking at you. Isn't that right? So why am I the pig?"

Hall didn't really want to listen to them get into the debate he could see they were obviously headed to. "OK, OK, never mind any of that, you two. So what's her face look like? I'm not you, I can't identify people by their ass and chest size."

Hyde continued laughing. "World might be a better place if we all could."

Charlotte looked up at the sky and rolled her eyes. "Oh. My—"

Hall quickly stepped in again. "OK, can we please get back on track here? What does her face look like?"

"Oh," Hyde replied. "I dunno, man, who notices stuff like that?"

"You only notice the good stuff, right?" Charlotte asked.

Hyde shrugged. "Whatever floats one's boat, right?"

"I'm gonna float—"

Hall sighed, unable to get the pair back on track. "Can you please just tell me what the woman's face looks like?"

"Uh, I dunno, man, I mean, she's got a face."

Charlotte burst out with a fake laugh. "Wow, that's really good. She's got a face."

"Hey, listen, lady—"

"What color hair does she have?" Hall asked. "Eye color?"

"Eyes? Listen, man, you're barking up the wrong tree there. I ain't never seen her eyes long enough to know what color they are. Not when there's so much else to see."

Hall put his hand back on his girlfriend's arm to prevent her from going off again, wanting to conclude this conversation as quickly as possible. "Hair?"

"Uh, I think it's black. Yeah, black."

"Are you sure?" Charlotte asked in a mocking fashion.

"Pretty sure. It's kinda long, like to the mid-part of her back. I only really remember 'cause she's got this thing when she's on stage where she looks back, and you're really only looking at—"

"We don't wanna know!"

"Oh. Just thought I'd—"

"No, we don't care."

"Well, you might be interested in this," Hyde said, looking at Hall.

"No, he's not!"

Hyde smiled. "Oh, that's cool. I see who's got the pants in your relationship."

"It's not about who's got the pants," Charlotte said, more than slightly irritated. "It's called having a loving relationship with an equal partner. You might wanna try it sometime."

Hyde made a face, not really caring about all that. "Uh, yeah."

"When is she usually working?" Hall asked.

"Dude, I don't know. I don't have her on speed dial or anything. I'm not one of those cats who are at those places all the time and am on a first name basis with everybody. Yeah, I might go down there once a week or something, but that's about all I can tell you. Maybe she's there tonight, maybe she's not. You're gonna have to find that stuff out for yourselves."

"Why didn't you tell us about this girl and Ripper before?"

"Cause you didn't ask before. Listen, man, I ain't in the business of just blindly giving away information to anyone who wants it. If you got something specific on your mind, you ask. If I know, and there's some green bills behind it, I might tell ya. That's it. I just don't go around the neighborhood flapping my gums to every Tom, Dick, and Harry that comes along. You've got to ask for the information you want."

"So you go to this place every week?" Charlotte asked.

"Yeah," Hyde proudly said. "Helps me unwind, if you know what I mean."

"Ew, that's so disgusting."

"If you go there tonight, let me know how you like it."

"You're so gross."

"You better watch yourself. They might try to recruit you or something. I could see you working there."

"I would sooner cut my arm off and jump into a snake pit with a bunch of cobras."

"Hey, whatever gets you off."

"Do you ever... wait a minute. If you go there every week, that means the money we're giving him, he's blowing it at some strip club?"

Hyde couldn't contain the huge smile on his face. "Nice knowing where your money's going, isn't it?"

"I'm not giving him money just so he can blow it on tits and ass!"

"What do you want me to spend it on? A library membership?"

"Try some food and clothes for your kids or something. And don't you have a girlfriend or something?"

"Yeah, why?"

"And she just lets you go to these places every week?! She's OK with it?"

"Listen, it ain't about whether she's cool with it or not," Hyde replied. "It's about what I want to do. I'm the man, I wear the pants, I say what I'm gonna do, and she'll have to live with it."

"Oh, you're just a peach, aren't you?"

"Some people think so."

"Even a blind person could tell what a pathetic piece of—"

Hall, tired of the bickering, grabbed Charlotte by the arm, pulling her down the steps. She stumbled a little, but didn't fight her boyfriend moving her. That didn't mean she was done talking to Hyde, though. She continued telling him what she thought of him even while Hall was taking her away. Hyde actually thought it was funny and kept smiling and laughing, even though he was being insulted the whole time. He got a kick out of other people thinking that way about him. It didn't bother him a bit.

When they finally got back to the car, Hall got his girlfriend in the passenger seat, then went around to the driver's side. Once he was inside, he looked at Charlotte, who was still mumbling to herself as she looked out the window. Hall smiled at her, thinking it was cute how agitated the man made her. He rarely saw her get so upset. Charlotte turned her head, noticing her boyfriend's gaze.

"Can you believe that guy? What a jerk!"

"Charlotte—"

"I mean, how do people live like that?"

"Charlotte—"

"I mean, it's just pathetic."

"Charlotte—"

"And I can't believe we're giving him money to ogle at women like that."

"Charlotte!"

"What?"

"It's done. You can let go now."

"It's just... he's such a..."

"Yeah, we know what he is," Hall said. "We don't have to like him. Or live with him. Or hang out with him. Or be buddies with him. All we have to do is get the right information out of him. That's all."

"But we're—"

"Don't think about anything else. As long as we get the right information, and he's been right on the money so far, that's what we're after. Right?"

Charlotte sighed, hating to admit it. "Yeah."

Hall looked up the strip club on his phone, finding the address as well as its hours of operation.

"Do we really have to go to a strip club?" Charlotte asked, not wanting to see what she knew she was going to see.

"You don't have to go. I can go by myself."

"Oh no, you're not! If you think I'm gonna let you go to one of those places by yourself, you've got another thing coming."

Dark Day

"Why? Don't you trust me?"

"It's not that. Of course I trust you. I just don't want you to see them... doing all these things, looking like that... and then be... you know, come home to boring old me."

Hall looked at her and smiled. He then touched her chin with his thumb and index finger, rubbing it gently. He picked her head up to look at him. "Listen, the only thing I would think about in a place like that, is that I would worry I'd have to fight all the guys off who were wondering how I got such a beautiful woman like you. 'Cause you'd obviously be the prettiest girl in the room."

Charlotte smiled at him. "You're sweet," she said, before planting a kiss on his lips. "Just make sure you walk in there with your eyes closed."

"How am I going to do that?"

"I'll put my hands over your eyes and I'll tell you where to go."

"I don't think that'll work."

"Oh, it'll work. Believe me, I'll make it work."

17

Hall and Charlotte arrived at the Hot Stuff strip club a couple hours after it opened. The club opened at six o'clock, but Hall called before they went there, just to make sure Candy was on the schedule for the night. The last thing either of them wanted, especially Charlotte, was to get there only to find out the woman wasn't working that night. Luckily, she was, but she wasn't scheduled to appear until nine o'clock.

They got to the club right at nine, assuming she wouldn't get on stage right away, not that they knew for sure. But they figured they wouldn't miss her even if she was. As soon as they walked in, Charlotte put her hands over her boyfriend's eyes.

"Really, Charlotte? I thought you were joking."

"Nope. I wasn't."

"I can't see."

"That's the point."

"Charlotte. I've got to be able to see. I swear I won't look at the stage."

"Promise?"

"I promise."

Charlotte removed her hands from Hall's eyes. As soon as Hall could see again, his eyes were directed right to the stage, where he could see a rather well-endowed woman with no top on dancing around a pole.

"You promised you wouldn't look!"

"But that's the way I was looking already!" Hall replied. "You should've turned me around first."

Hall honestly wasn't that interested in what was happening on stage and looked around the room, trying to see if Candy was there somewhere. The room was only about half-full, which surprised them a little. They thought it would have been a full house.

"She must be backstage somewhere."

"I'm sure we can't get back there," Charlotte said. "Not that I think I'd want to."

"Well, we gotta talk to her somehow."

"Maybe wait for her to come out."

"I assume they don't go out through the front. Probably have a back door with security to make sure none of the ladies are touched."

"Like they would have a problem with that."

"Look, they're just people trying to make a living."

Charlotte rolled her eyes. "You're such a pushover. I'm sure there are other ways to do it besides flaunting yourselves for a bunch of chauvinistic men."

"What makes you think they're chauvinistic?"

"Please. Have you looked around the room yet?"

"OK. Instead of standing here and judging people, how 'bout we actually see if we can find this Candy girl."

Charlotte shook her head and gave him a ridiculous-looking kind of face. "Really? Candy girl? Please tell me you didn't do that on purpose?"

"Actually, I kind of did."

"That makes it worse."

"Just trying to inject some humor."

Before moving, Charlotte put her hand on her boyfriend's arm, something striking her mind. "I just thought of something."

Hall opened his mouth, ready to let loose with something sarcastic, like that would be a first, but decided to just let it go. It probably wasn't worth the look he'd get. "Oh? Anything interesting?"

"What if Ripper was here?"

"What?"

"Well, if Candy is his girl, wouldn't it be possible he was here?"

Hall immediately started looking around the room. He hadn't thought about it up to that point, but he couldn't rule it out. He thought it kind of strange watching your girlfriend, or acquaintance if they weren't that formal, dance on a stage for other men and women, but to each their own.

"Only problem is we don't really know what he looks like."

"What do you mean?" Charlotte asked. "We got the description from Thurmond when he was talking to Bradham at the station."

"That could've fit anybody. He's not tall, not short, around six foot tall. Medium build, long hair and a beard."

"So let's look for someone that looks like that."

"If Ripper's as smart as I think he is, that's probably not what he actually looks like. Hair can be cut, facial hair can be shaved. I doubt if he actually has long hair or a beard."

"Master of deception. Almost like that Rankin guy."

The thought occurred to him before, but for some reason, it really struck him now. A guy who wasn't what he appeared to be. A mastermind who had other people do the illegal acts for him, then when he didn't need them, or they posed some kind of threat that might expose him, he got rid of them. Ripper sure sounded like he operated on Rankin's MO. Maybe they were evil twin brothers. Or maybe they were the same guy.

Another ten minutes went by, and tired of waiting, they were about to start asking around about Candy. It turned out they didn't have to, though. The music changed, and different colored lights shone down brightly on the stage. Everyone looked to the stage, seeing Candy hop onto it, immediately going into one of her numbers. After a minute of dancing about, Candy's top finally came off, much to the happiness of the customers, who started hooting and hollering.

"Pigs," Charlotte muttered.

Hall watched the woman on stage, though he was more than uncomfortable in doing so. It felt kind of dirty to him. Not that he especially had a problem with the profession, or anyone who was there watching. To each their own, he thought. But with Charlotte next to him, it just didn't feel right. Even if Charlotte wasn't next to him, it wouldn't have felt right. Not that he would have been there to begin with, because he would never have visited one of these places if it wasn't work-related. A few minutes later, after Candy's routine was up, she left the stage and went back to the dressing room.

"Look at all those slobs just throwing money at her," Charlotte said. "Unreal. Just because she's got big boobs."

"Guess it's like they say. Use it if you got it."

Charlotte gave him a look, at which Hall just threw up his hands. "I mean, don't these people have anything better to do with their money then just throw it at some woman who probably wouldn't be caught dead with any of them anyway?"

"I guess it's just the way some people relax."

"Why don't they try it with a real woman?"

"I'm pretty sure she is a real woman."

"I don't mean it like that. I mean a real woman, like, who is with them, cares about them, stuff like that. Not someone who just takes their clothes off then takes their money."

"Different people have different hobbies."

"This is not a hobby."

Hall shrugged, not really caring to debate the topic. He was much more interested in getting back to see Candy, that way they could question her and get out of there. They walked over to a side door, which led to the hallway and the dressing room that the girls got changed in backstage. There was a big, muscular man guarding the door. Hall looked at him and sighed, hoping he wasn't one of those guys who were quick to a fight. Not that he couldn't have taken the muscled-up man, but he knew he'd probably take several shots in the process. And he really wasn't in the mood for that. Once they got closer, the bouncer put his arm up to stop them from moving any further.

"Nobody's allowed back there," the bouncer said. "Only authorized personnel."

"Oh, we're not looking to, uh, do anything," Hall said. "We just wanna talk to Candy."

"You a friend of hers?"

"Well, uh, no, not quite."

"Well then, you ain't getting back there."

"Then could you have her come out here?"

The guard shook his head. "The girls aren't allowed to fraternize with the customers."

"We're not customers. We just wanna talk to her."

Feeling like they were getting nowhere, Charlotte stepped in, sounding as forceful as Hall had ever heard her.

"Listen up, you. I saw a few bags of coke being passed around out there, and I don't mean soda. Unless you want the cops down here in the next three minutes, tell Candy to come out and talk to us."

"You guys feds?"

"No, we're not," Hall answered. "Look, all we wanna do is talk to Candy. We can do it out here at one of the tables if you prefer, so we're in full view of everyone."

"No, management wouldn't like that. People see her talking to someone, then everyone's gonna want to get their hands on her."

"So what do you suggest?"

"Cops?" Charlotte asked. "We got a detective on speed dial."

The guard put his hands up, hoping to calm them down. Police being there wasn't good for anybody. Especially the health of the business. He sighed and took a look around, making sure there weren't any eyes looking on them.

"OK, listen, I can take you into a back room where you can talk to her. It's not much, but there's a table and a couple folding chairs. I'll tell her you guys are here."

"Tell her it's about a friend of hers," Hall said. "Jack Ripper. She'll know what we mean."

"Ripper." The guard's reaction to the name indicated that he knew him. Or at least had heard about him.

"You know him?"

The guard thought for a few more seconds. "Maybe. Is that the guy with the shaved head, light brown hair? Kinda like yours."

"Could be," Hall said. "Seen him here often?"

"Just with Candy a few times."

"Where at?" Hall asked. He then pointed to the tables where the customers sat. "Out there somewhere?"

"No, he was allowed backstage sometimes. Boyfriends, or girlfriends, you know how it is these days, they're allowed back there with them sometimes."

"Oh? Was he here often?"

"Uh, maybe a handful of times. Five or so."

Hall smiled. "That's a handful."

"What would they do?" Charlotte asked. "Anything in particular?"

"You know, talk, hangout, do other things."

"What other things?"

"Well, we got a few other rooms back there, kind of like the one you'll be going in. There's a table, some couches, that way the girls can just relax between performances if they want, or they'll play cards, have a few shots."

"Drugs?" Hall asked.

"Eh, a few of them do. Nothing hard as far as I know. A little weed or something. And if their boyfriends are there... sometimes they do a little extra." The bouncer laughed, all of them getting his meaning.

It took all that Charlotte had not to tell him how gross he sounded. But considering the place she was in, she didn't think it would go over too well.

"Ever hear what they were talking about?" Hall asked.

"Nah, not really. I don't spend too much time back there. I'm mostly here on the door."

"Yes, well, I can see why. You seem like you're good at your job."

With nothing else to discuss, the guard opened the door, then led the pair back down the hallway. It was a narrow hallway and looked like it hadn't been cleaned in some time. As they were walking, one of the girls came out of the dressing room and passed them. They all stood to the side to give her enough room to pass. She wasn't wearing much. It looked like a black bikini, with quite a bit hanging out of it at both ends. As she passed Hall, she gave him a smile and winked. She then pretended to trip and fell into him, pressing her chest into his, forcing his back against the wall.

"Oh, excuse me," she said. "I must've tripped over something."

Hall gulped and took his hands off the woman's waist. "Quite all right."

"Sorry."

"No problem."

"My name's Tiffany. What's yours?"

Charlotte was not going to have any of that. She knew exactly what game the woman was playing. She stormed over to her and took her hand off his arm. "His name is Taken. Thanks." She then pulled him away from her, looking back to see the woman still staring at him. "The nerve of her!" She shook her head, still steaming. "Yeah, I just happened to trip over the floor. Over air. Uh huh."

Hall smiled, getting a kick out of seeing his girlfriend get upset like that. They caught back up to the guard, who took them into another room. He was right. There wasn't much to it. Concrete walls, an old beaten down card table in the middle of the room, with some rusty folding chairs on each end of it. There was even a green couch against the wall that looked like it had seen better days. The stuffing was beginning to come out of it.

"I guess that's where the dancers and their significant others have some fun," Hall said, smiling and pointing over to the couch. He knew the statement was sure to get a rise out of his girlfriend.

"Eww. That's so gross. I'm so not sitting there."

Hall laughed, egging her on even more. "I mean, what's the worst that could have happened there?"

"You really are trying to make me throw up, aren't you?"

"Maybe we could do a few things on it while we're waiting."

"Ew. I love you and all, but there isn't any way I'm sitting on that thing. There is nothing in the world you could give me that would make me sit, or worse, lay on it. Nothing."

"Nothing?"

"I wouldn't care if it started shooting up gold coins," Charlotte replied. "You couldn't get me on that thing for anything."

"That'd be an interesting sight. Shooting up cold coins."

They stood there for a few minutes, pacing around, waiting for Candy to appear. Charlotte seemed short on patience.

"Where is this woman? Don't have all night to wait."

Hall smiled at her. "What's the hurry?"

"I just want to get out of this place. And the sooner we can do that, the better I'll like it."

18

Hall and Charlotte waited close to ten minutes, still without a sign or word from Candy. The thought occurred to them that maybe she wasn't going to show at all.

"You don't think she took off, do you?"

"Why would she?" Hall asked.

"I don't know. A couple strange people come into her work asking about Ripper, maybe she figures something's up, doesn't wanna talk, slips out the back door while we're waiting in here."

Hall couldn't deny that it was possible. But he didn't think it was likely. At least he hoped not. There really was no reason for her to run without knowing what was happening. Charlotte was so wrapped up in wondering what was going on that she actually sat down. On a folding chair, not the couch. Not that she felt all that much better on the chair, but how much fooling around could someone do on a folding chair? Regardless, she didn't have to worry much longer. About a minute later, their heads snapped to the door when they heard the knob start to turn. The door opened, and the first thing either of them saw was the long, bare, tanned legs of a woman. They belonged to Candy. She looked at the two of them apprehensively, wondering what they wanted with her.

"Nice to see you… again," Hall said.

Charlotte was somewhat relieved, not only that the woman showed up, but that she at least wasn't half-naked as well. Candy had a burgundy-colored robe on, and while it wasn't especially long, barely covering her bottom, at least she wasn't popping out of her top.

"Oh, see my show out there?" Candy asked.

"Uh, yes, yes, we did," Charlotte replied.

"What'd you think?"

"It was… nice," Hall answered.

"Just nice?"

"Well…"

Candy then looked at Charlotte and smiled, thinking the guy didn't want to say how much he enjoyed it in front of his girlfriend, if that's what she was. "Oh, I get it. Sure."

"We're not here to talk about your performance," Charlotte said.

"Yeah, that's what Gary said. Something about Jack?"

"That's right," Hall said. "Do you know a Jack Ripper?"

"Of course, why? What's going on?"

"We're looking for him, and we were hoping you could help us find him. We understand you guys are a thing."

"Not like that. I mean, we're not exclusive or anything. We just... have a good time together. But that's about it. We're not a couple."

"It's OK. Where can we find him?"

Candy carefully looked at the two of them. Hall seemed to have the appearance of a cop. Not Charlotte, though. That's what threw her off. "You guys cops or something?"

"No, we're private investigators."

"That's almost as bad."

"We think Ripper's tied up with some things, and we wanna find him."

"And you think I can tell you where he is?"

"Can't you?"

Candy shook her head. "Nope. Sorry. Don't know where he is."

"You mean you won't tell us?" Charlotte said.

"I mean, I can't. I don't know where he's at. Simple as that."

"So you don't know where he lives, where he hangs out, nothing?"

"Never been to his place. He would always meet me

here, then we'd either go out somewhere or back to my place."

"How long have you been seeing him?" Hall asked.

"About six months?"

"Any particular places he likes to hang out?"

"Different place every time."

"What do you know about him?"

"Just the basics. Not much. Men like Jack, they don't like to divulge too much."

"And you just go along with it?" Charlotte asked.

"Listen, honey, it wasn't anything serious. I didn't need to know all the details about his past or what he planned in the future. We had a good time together, did some cool things, that was enough for me."

"Ever hear him talking about his business?" Hall asked. "What'd he do for a living?"

"Never said much about it. Just that he travelled a lot for it. Some type of sales thing."

"That's it?"

"About as much as I know. Why? What do you think he's done?"

"We're not sure. Maybe nothing. Just wanted to talk to him about a case we were working on. Thought he might be able to help us out with it."

"Oh. Well, whatever it is, I doubt he would help."

"Why?"

"Jack's not the talkative type."

Hall nodded, getting the feeling they were wasting their time. Either Candy really didn't know much, or

Ripper had trained her in how to answer questions, especially about him.

"So you never heard him say anything, do anything, something that you thought was strange at the time?"

"No, not really." Candy looked at the wall for a moment, thinking. "Uh, well, there was this one time."

"When?"

"It was maybe a month ago. Three weeks. Something like that. Anyway, we were in here, and he got a phone call. He walked over there to the couch. I got the feeling he was trying to talk low so I couldn't hear him."

"What was being said?" Hall asked.

"I couldn't hear all of it. Something about insurance. At first, I assumed he was talking to his insurance agent or something, but then he got a little mad, and it didn't sound like that was it."

"Did you hear what he got mad about?"

"Don't know the details. All I heard was something about... if that bitch doesn't get in line, we'll have to take care of her, there's too much money at stake, blah blah blah. That was pretty much it."

Hall looked at Charlotte. "Learson."

"Who?" Candy asked.

"Nothing. How'd he seem after that?"

"Agitated. Angry. It took him a few minutes to cool off. Looked like he had a lot on his mind. I asked him what it was all about, but he didn't want to say. Just blew it off. Said it was nothing."

"Any of the times you ever met with him, he ever have anyone else with him?"

"What, you mean like another girl or something?"

"Anyone," Hall replied. "Man, woman, whatever."

Candy shook her head. "No, he's pretty much a loner." She then stopped for a few seconds, remembering another encounter. "Wait, there was this one time. We were at a restaurant eating dinner, it was around eight, nine, something like that. Anyway, he excused himself and got up real suddenly and went outside. I looked out the window and saw him talking to someone. Don't know what it was about, though. He didn't say, and I didn't want to ask. Figured it was his business."

"Could you describe the guy he was talking to?"

As Candy described the man she saw, it sounded familiar. Hall reached inside his pocket and removed a picture of Coulson, showing it to her.

"Is that him?" Hall asked.

"Yeah. That's the guy."

"You're sure?"

"Oh, I'm positive. He's got one of those mean faces you never forget."

"When was this?"

"Last week. Who is he?" Candy asked.

Hall looked at Charlotte, not sure if he should say. But in the end, he thought it better to tell the truth.

Especially since Candy was trying to be helpful. Though initially Hall thought maybe she was trying to evade their questions, now it seemed she was just being honest. She didn't know much. Or maybe thought she didn't know much. She was telling the truth as she knew it.

"His name is Remi Coulson. He's a hired killer."

Candy's eyes almost popped out. "A hired killer?"

"Surprised?"

"Uh, yeah! I mean, it's not every day you hear things like that."

"I bet."

"Wait, are you sure about that? I mean, if he's really a hired killer, why would he be hanging around Jack?"

Hall raised his eyebrows. "Maybe because he's the one who hired him."

"What?! That's crazy! You think Jack and this guy are mixed up in something?"

"Actually, we do."

"That's nuts. Jack isn't a killer."

"How do you know? You say you don't know much about him."

"Well, I don't. It's just that... I dunno, he just doesn't seem the type. He seems... I dunno. Normal. Very intelligent, very smart."

"A very smart man is the person we're looking for. He's the one who engineered all this."

"All what?"

"An insurance scam," Hall said. "Fraud. It involved

an insurance executive, a few small-time criminals, and this guy." Hall held up Coulson's picture again. "You know what they all have in common? They're all dead. All three of them, four if you include a woman Coulson was seeing. Four people dead. Know what the common link is?" Hall held up Coulson's picture once more. "They were all killed by this guy."

"That's incredible."

"And then you tell us he was seen talking to Ripper. You overhear Ripper talking about some insurance issue, where he's getting mad, telling someone that someone else needs to be taken care of. Good chance that someone was Carly Learson. She was one of the people involved in the scam. She was also the first one found dead."

Candy shook her head, having a hard time processing it all. Though she wasn't especially close to Ripper, he didn't seem like that kind of person to her. He never seemed threatening or the violent type. And she'd been around a few guys that wouldn't have shocked her if they'd been arrested for murder. But this threw her for a loop.

"I don't, um... I don't know what to say," Candy said.

"You know where we can find him?" Hall asked. "If there's more people involved in this that we don't know about yet, they're probably gonna be found dead too. Unless we can stop it."

Candy wiped her face, looking a little shaken by

the news. "No. No, I don't. I was telling you the truth earlier. I don't... I don't know where he lives or anything."

"Maybe he gave you a clue or something? Something that didn't make you think twice before, but now would make sense?"

Candy looked down at the floor, shaking her head, nothing coming to her. "I just can't think of anything."

"When's the next time you're supposed to meet with Ripper?" Charlotte asked.

"No time soon. A few days ago he came in here, telling me he was going away for a while. Said he was going away on business."

"Did he say where?"

"No. Just like always, didn't say much."

"That was it?" Hall asked. "He just came in, said he was leaving, then left?"

"No, he came in, we came in this room, we talked for a few minutes, said it would be the last time we saw each other for a while, then we wound up on the couch for a while, then that was it. He left, I went on stage, haven't seen or heard from him since."

"When was that?"

"Four or five days ago."

Hall and Charlotte looked at each other for a few moments, both waiting for the other to ask a question. Nothing seemed to come to them, though. Then something occurred to Hall. He looked at Candy, thinking she might be in trouble.

"Ripper knows where you live?"

"Yeah, we've been there a bunch of times," Candy answered.

"Live there with anyone?"

"No, I live alone. Why are you asking?"

"Because he's been tying off loose ends," Hall replied. "I think you might be one."

"What? What are you saying?"

"Everyone who's known about this insurance thing he's got going on has been eliminated. Coulson was apparently dating someone who was also eliminated. Probably because he didn't want anyone identifying him. Now that leaves just you."

"What are you saying? That Jack's going to kill me?"

"I would be surprised if he did it himself. Coulson, on the other hand. He'd be the one getting the order."

"I can't believe that. I don't even know anything!"

"You know there's some type of insurance thing going on," Hall said. "You heard him talking about it. He knows that. Now he's wrapping things up."

Candy shook her head vigorously, refusing to believe that the man she knew would do something like that. "No. I don't believe it."

"You can. You just won't."

"If he was going to do something like that, don't you think he would've tried it already? Why would I still be here?"

"You weren't the highest priority. Others who knew more, they came first."

"No. No. No."

"Are you denying it because you really don't believe it, or because you don't want to believe it."

"It's not true."

"Suit yourself. I would suggest not going home for a few days. Maybe contact the police for protection."

"I don't need protection. And I haven't been home in like a week."

"Why?"

"I had a friend come into town from Houston. She had an extra bed in her hotel room, so I've just been hanging out with her all week."

That was it, Hall thought. That's why they hadn't made an attempt on her before now. She hadn't been home. Though they knew where she worked, they wouldn't want to do it in a public place, with so many people around. They would wait until Candy got somewhere quiet.

"Have you worked all week?" Hall asked. "Since your friend arrived, I mean?"

"No, this is my first night since she got here. She left earlier today."

That explained even more to Hall. If Candy hadn't been home for a few days, it was likely they would have tried to tail her from the club, figuring out where she was going if she wasn't going home. And they would have taken her out then. That made Hall think that if they were thinking about taking the woman out, they would do it soon. Possibly even tonight.

"Anything else you wanna add?" Hall asked.

Candy shook her head. "Nope. I've told you all I know."

"Well, thanks for your time."

"Yep." Though Candy said she didn't believe what she was being told, the worried look on her face told Hall otherwise. A lot was going through her mind now. That much was obvious.

"Make sure you keep your eyes open."

"I will."

"And think about what I said about that protection."

Candy looked up at him and nodded, the first indication she gave that she actually was thinking about her safety. Hall and Charlotte walked out of the room, going back into the main part of the club. Before leaving, they took another look around, making sure that Coulson wasn't in there already. They didn't believe Ripper would be there, but there wasn't anybody matching his description, anyway. They were about to leave, then Hall walked over to the guard again, taking out the picture of Coulson to show him.

"You ever see this guy in here before?"

The guard took a careful look at the photo. "Uh, yeah, yeah, I've seen him. He's been here a couple of times."

"You remember when?"

"Yeah, just this week actually. He was here maybe three or four days ago. Then he was here again last night."

"He talk to anyone in here? Ask any questions?"

"Not as far as I know. I saw him sitting at a table, having some drinks, just watching the girls on stage. Didn't cause any trouble or anything."

Hall put the picture back in his pocket. "Listen, where do the girls leave when they're done? Front or back?"

"Back."

"Alone?"

"I can't really tell you…"

"Look, the reason I ask is that I think Candy might be in some trouble."

"Candy? Why?"

"This guy in the photo, he's a real bad guy," Hall said. "I think he's planning on doing something to her. I wanna make sure she gets home safe."

"That's good of you."

"So is there protection for the girls when they leave?"

"There's a guard on the back door. He sees to it that the girls get to their car without being bothered. Every now and then you'll have a knucklehead who sees one of the girls, thinks he's got a shot to hook up with them or something, then waits for them out back."

"What time is Candy's shift over?"

"She's usually here till midnight."

Hall nodded and slapped the guard on the arm. "Thanks for all the help."

"Hey, if that creep's after Candy, you make sure she gets home all right?"

"I'll do my best."

Hall and Charlotte then went back to their car and waited. And they would have a long wait.

"We're just gonna sit here until midnight?" Charlotte asked.

"That's the plan."

"But they might not even show up tonight."

"Oh, I think they'll show up."

"What makes you think so?"

"Coulson's been here twice this week. I don't think there's any doubt he's looking for her. And I'm willing to bet that at some point yesterday, he asked when Candy was working next."

"But the guard said he didn't notice him talking to anyone."

"That he noticed. I'm sure his eyes weren't pinned on Coulson the entire time. He's guarding the door, making sure the girls come in and out…"

"He's not that busy."

"Still, if the guy's just sitting there minding his business, he's not gonna pay much attention to him. He's gonna be watching the guys who are loud and rowdy. Not to mention the girls on the stage, which I'm sure he sneaks a peek at every now and then."

"You think Ripper will show up? Or just Coulson?"

"I don't think there's any chance Ripper's showing up. He's hired Coulson for a reason. He'll let him do it."

"I think we should call Bradham and let him know," Charlotte said.

"Yeah, I think you're right."

"Especially since he's already taken you before." Charlotte smiled, not able to resist another dig at her boyfriend.

Hall lowered his head and put the palm of his hand over his forehead. "I'm really never gonna live this down."

19

Bradham was able to get to the club not too long after being called. He wasn't able to spare any more men from other assignments though, so it was just him. He did have a patrol car cruise around Candy's apartment to look for signs of trouble, just in case Coulson was waiting there instead. Hall and Charlotte were in the front parking lot, keeping an eye out. Bradham was on the next street over, parked along the street, but it still gave him a good vantage point to behind the Hot Stuff building. He could see when the girls came out. The two cars talked to each other almost the entire time while they were waiting.

"You know, you don't exactly have strong evidence that Coulson's gonna be here."

"All the pieces seem to fit," Hall said. "Why else would he be hanging around the last few days?"

"Maybe he got bored."

"You know as well as I do what he's doing."

"But that doesn't mean he's gonna do it tonight," Bradham said.

"They're not gonna want to let this linger. It's gonna be soon."

"I hope so. I can't be having stakeouts every night indefinitely."

They continued to wait until midnight, seeing no trace of Coulson before then. He didn't go into the building; they didn't notice him walking around; they didn't see the same type of car cruising up and down the street, there was none of that. It was just another quiet night. It was 12:10 a.m. when Candy finally left the building.

"Got her in my sights," Bradham said, sitting up at attention in case he had to move quickly. Candy was escorted to her car by the guard, no problems in sight. "All clear so far."

Once Candy got on the road, Bradham followed her, though not too closely. Hall and Charlotte stayed behind for a few minutes, just to see if someone else was following too. No one did. At least not that they could see. Once they were satisfied that Coulson wasn't there, they headed in the direction of Candy's apartment too, a few minutes behind the detective. It was about a twenty-minute drive to the apartment. By the time they got there, Bradham was already out of his vehicle, standing by the driver's side door, waiting for his friends to arrive. Hall and Charlotte both got out of the car after parking next to the detective.

"What's going on?" Hall asked.

"Nothing's going on," Bradham replied. "That's the point. Nothing's going on. I just talked to the patrol car that's been driving around here. Hasn't seen a thing out of the ordinary."

"Is that really surprising? You think a guy like Coulson doesn't know how to keep out of sight when the black and white rolls along?"

"I've also driven by here. There's nothing unusual. There's nobody sitting in a car waiting, nobody walking around, there's nothing here." Hall looked frustrated, sighing as he looked around the property. "Listen, you've done all you can. Your reasoning's been sound, your logic has been good, everything fits."

"Except it doesn't."

"Like I said, doesn't mean it's happening tonight. They might be thinking someone's watching her too, so they're giving her some space. Remember Thurmond? They left him alone at first, too. It wasn't until after we picked him up that they killed him. Maybe it's gonna be the same with her. Maybe they figure there's nothing to fear unless we talk to her."

Hall nodded, acknowledging the possibility. "And maybe I just screwed it up by asking her questions back at the club."

Bradham slapped his friend on the arm, somewhat sympathetically. "Can't worry about that. You were just going where the clues took you. Go home. Get some rest."

"Maybe I'll stay here for a while. Just to make sure."

"Brandon, you can't follow this woman twenty-four seven. Go home. Get some rest. You look tired. You'll need to use that brain tomorrow to figure out another angle. Can't do that when you're dead tired and can't think."

Hall nodded again, hearing him, though he wasn't quite sure whether he was going to listen or not. Not yet. He still was having trouble getting it out of his mind that Coulson was nearby, even though there was no proof of it.

"Anybody check inside?"

"Brandon, you told her to come to us, you offered her protection, she refused on both counts, that's all you can do. Unfortunately, that's part of this business. Sometimes, the people who need your help don't want it. And you've got to be able to accept that and move on. Whatever happens from here on out, it's not on you." Bradham then got back in his car. "Accept it and move on."

Hall looked at him, appearing to understand, though not quite willing to accept it himself.

Bradham looked to Charlotte. "Get him home. You too. You've done all you can. You both need to get some rest. Come back at it again in the morning and figure out your next step from there."

Charlotte looked at her boyfriend and rubbed his arm, then back at the detective. "I'll try."

Bradham started up his car, then pulled out of the parking lot. They watched him leave, his brake lights fluttering as he stopped at a light, then moved on again once it turned green. Once he was completely out of sight, Charlotte looked at her boyfriend, obvious that something was still on his mind.

"Did I misread everything?" Hall asked. "Maybe she's not in any trouble. Maybe I was just making it up because it sounded plausible."

"It all made sense."

"But did it make enough sense? I mean, Coulson's not here. Hasn't tried anything."

"But that doesn't mean he won't."

"Bradham's right, though. We can't stay here and protect her forever."

"Brandon, it's like he said. We offered her help. She didn't want it. There's nothing more we can do."

"Maybe we should go in and check her apartment, make sure he's not hiding in there somewhere."

"She's been home for ten minutes now," Charlotte said. "Don't you think she'd know it by now if there was?"

Hall slapped the side of his leg in frustration. "Probably."

"Let's do what Bradham said. Let's go home, get some rest, then figure out what to do in the morning."

"Let's just stick around another hour or two. Make sure nothing happens."

Charlotte sighed, not that she was unhappy about staying. She was fine with whatever he wanted to do. But she could tell it was starting to eat at him, and that was upsetting to her. They got back in the car, set to keep an eye on Candy's first-floor apartment for a few hours. They sank into the seats of their car, ready to be in there for the long haul. Hall kept his eyes focused on the sliding glass doors that led into Candy's apartment, periodically checking the parking lot for any cars that might pull in or people that might be walking along.

Charlotte also kept her eyes on the apartment for the most part, though after half an hour, she pulled out her phone and started reading, as she sometimes did at night. Reading usually made her tired and helped her fall asleep. It was just as true on this night as any other. About twenty minutes after she began, her head slumped to the side, resting up against the glass window, the phone slipping out of her hands.

Hall looked over at her and smiled. He loved her. He knew this wasn't where she wanted to be, but she was willing to be there, without even the tiniest complaint, because she wanted to support him and be with him. The gesture wasn't lost on him. He reached over and put his hand on her face, rubbing her cheek. He put his hand in hers, then lifted it up to his face, kissing the top of it gently.

"I love you," he softly told her.

Hall then reached down on the floor to grab her phone, putting it in the middle console. At some point over the next hour, Hall joined his girlfriend and fell asleep, his head leaning back against the headrest. It would be a short rest for him, however. He had slept for maybe thirty minutes when he suddenly woke up, looking around like he wasn't sure what was going on. He wiped the sleep from his eyes, still a little groggy. He focused his eyes on Candy's apartment. Nothing looked out of the ordinary. Everything looked the same as it did before.

Hall took a deep breath, then got out of his car, not wanting to fall asleep again. He figured the cool night air would help to wake him up. He gently closed the door so he didn't wake his girlfriend. He leaned up against the car and stretched his arms out. He yawned a couple of times. Then, suddenly, his head snapped toward Candy's apartment. He heard it. Gunshots. Two of them. There was no doubt where they came from. He looked a little closer at the double sliding glass doors and saw what looked like a broken piece of glass toward the end, hardly noticeable unless you were staring at it. The door looked like it was open just a hair.

Hall immediately started running toward the apartment. His heart started beating heavily, feeling as if it was going to pop out of his chest. A wave of anxiousness came over his body, fearful of what he was going to find once he got there. He ran across the hard pavement, his knees and legs feeling so heavy, like they were going to punch holes in the road surface. He jumped over the curb and onto the grass, Candy's apartment within range in a few more seconds.

Just then, the sliding door opened, and a dark figure emerged, dressed in all black. Hall recognized the man as Coulson. Hall ran straight for him, bracing himself for a high-impact collision. Coulson was surprised at seeing someone else there and stood still for a moment. It wasn't until Hall was almost on top of him that he recognized who he was. It was the same man he battled with back at Groshens' house. For a change, Coulson was paralyzed, unsure what to do as the man charged at him. He didn't have much of a chance to move anywhere, though. By the time Coulson came out of the apartment and saw Hall, only a few seconds had elapsed. Hardly enough time to process anything, other than trying to stiffen his body to make any impact not as severe.

It was no use. There was nothing Coulson could do to stop the raging bull that was charging at him. Upon reaching his target, Hall drove his shoulder into Coulson's gut, driving the two of them backwards. The force and weight of the two men went straight through the glass door, completely shattering it, pieces of glass falling on top of them as they fell to the carpeted floor inside the apartment.

Both men were stunned, hurt, cut, and bleeding. The impact of the collision made getting back to their feet a slow task for each of them. They were a little wobbly when they tried to stand up again, though the strength quickly returned to their systems, probably due to the rush of knowing each of their lives were in danger from the other. Coulson was the first to get back to his feet, Hall following not too far behind. Coulson, though, was able to get in the first blow, kicking his opponent in the face. Hall fell back to the ground, his hand falling on some glass, cutting his palm. He winced in pain, though he quickly shrugged it off, wanting to deliver some punishment of his own.

Coulson came over to him and hit Hall with a few punches to the face. Hand-to-hand combat wasn't Coulson's favorite thing to do, though, and he sought to end the fight sooner rather than later. He reached into his belt, putting his fingers on the handle of his gun. He took it out, and just as he pointed the barrel at his adversary's head, Hall rushed him, spearing him in the stomach once again. The gun flew out of Coulson's hand. The two wrested on the ground for a minute, each trying to get the upper hand, rolling on top of one another, trying to get a blow in that would give them the advantage. They both struggled to gain that advantage, though. They were pretty evenly matched in their contest.

Several more minutes went by and the two eventually got back to their feet, both able to get in a few blows on the other, but none so bad that the other lost control of the battle. They continued getting in some punches and kicks until their fight raged into the kitchen. They fell on top of the kitchen table, collapsing the wooden legs beneath their weight, both of them crashing to the floor. Both slow to get up, Coulson was the first to his feet, as Hall had gotten to his hands and knees. Coulson looked around for his gun, though he couldn't initially find it. He didn't have time to look for it either. Not with the other man getting back to his feet. Coulson needed to get out of there. He needed to escape. By whatever means possible.

Coulson saw a flower pot on top of the counter and picked it up, smashing it on top of Hall's head. The martial arts expert fell to the floor. This was his chance to escape, while Hall was still having a hard time getting up. Coulson started to look for his gun again, but then heard a voice from outside.

"Brandon!" Charlotte yelled. "Are you in there?!"

Coulson had no more time to waste. He had to leave. Now. He rushed out the newly opened sliding door, taking a quick peek at Charlotte as she approached, just to make sure she didn't have a weapon pointed at him. Another time, when he wasn't so pressed to leave, he probably would have gone after the woman, killing her for seeing his face leaving the scene of a crime. But Coulson knew he didn't have that kind of time. Not now. There was no telling how long Hall would be down for, and if Coulson sized up the toughness of his opponent properly, it wouldn't be long at all. Charlotte stopped in her tracks at the sight of Coulson, waiting for him to make the first move to determine what she was going to do. Luckily for her, he just started running. Running away from the apartment and toward his car, which was parked at the far end of the complex.

Charlotte waited a few moments before moving, wanting to make sure Coulson was a safe distance away before doing anything. She called Hall's name a few more times as she ran toward the apartment. Getting no answer, her heart started beating fast, her mind beginning to run away with thoughts she didn't want to think. By the time she stepped foot inside the apartment, she took light footsteps through the door, afraid of what she might find. She could feel the sweat forming on her hand and arms. Her heart was still racing, anxiety almost overcoming her. She looked at the mess on the floor, then saw Hall's legs moving in the kitchen, his feet extending past the wall. Charlotte ran into the room, kneeling down next to him as he clutched the back of his head and rolled over, finally sitting up.

"Are you OK?!"

Hall cleared his throat, still holding the back of his head. "Uh, yeah, yeah, I'm OK."

Charlotte looked at the cuts on his arms as well as his face. He certainly didn't look it. "You've got a funny way of showing it."

She put her arms all over his chest, stomach, and

legs, fearful that he might have been shot, since he did have some blood on his shirt. It was actually a mixture of his own blood as well as Coulson's, rolling around on top of each other had smeared the two of theirs together.

"I'm not shot," Hall said. "I'm fine. It's just some cuts from the glass."

"Do you know your name, where you're at?"

Hall looked at her and actually was able to smile. "I'm fine, Charlotte. I know my name, the date, what day it is, where I'm at, the color of the sky, all that. I'm OK."

"You might have a concussion."

Hall took a deep breath, then with his girlfriend's assistance, got back to his feet. He rolled his head around, along with his back, then his arms, trying to get loose again. In truth, his entire body ached at that point. And it probably would for a few more days.

"C'mon, let's get out of here," Charlotte said, not even thinking about anything else at that point.

Hall started walking, then stopped. "Wait. Candy."

"Oh my god, where is she?"

"I don't know. I heard the shots, that's why I came in."

They frantically started looking around the apartment. She wasn't in the kitchen or the living room. They went down the short hallway, coming across the bathroom first. She wasn't there. Then they went down to the bedroom, seeing her body lying on her back on the bed. Hall closed his eyes and sighed, while Charlotte turned her head away and buried it in her boyfriend's arm. They were too late. Candy was dead. It was the same as the others. One bullet in the chest, one more in the head.

Charlotte was able to pull herself away from Hall's arm for a minute. "I'll, uh, I'll call Bradham."

Hall nodded, not able to find any words. He felt like this was his fault. He knew Coulson was coming. He knew it. And he didn't stop it. He was out there in the parking lot, waiting for him to come, and Hall fell asleep. If he hadn't, if he'd have seen Coulson approach, Candy would still be alive. He never would have let Coulson get in to kill her. As Charlotte left the apartment to get her phone and call Bradham, Hall stood there at the edge of the bed, staring at Candy's body, feeling like he'd failed her. A couple minutes later, Charlotte came back in, seeing Hall standing in the same spot. He hadn't moved.

"It's not your fault."

"It is," Hall said. "I fell asleep. I woke up, heard the shots. Then I came in. If I'd been awake the entire time, I could have prevented this."

"You don't know that. What if you'd have fought first, then he broke away from you, then killed her?"

"Then it would still be my fault."

"Brandon, you can't think like that."

"It's the truth."

Charlotte's heart broke for him, knowing how hard

he was taking this. All she could do was try to convince him he was wrong about being responsible. She grabbed him by the arm and pulled him back.

"C'mon, let's wait outside."

Hall let her lead him outside, where they waited just outside the apartment, sitting on the ground with their backs to the wall. Charlotte put her arms around him and pulled him close, just holding him. It was all she could do.

20

Hall had been checked out by paramedics, and though they advised him to go to the hospital, he declined. He wasn't going anywhere while Coulson was still on the loose. Bradham was on the scene and already checked out the inside of the apartment, where the crime scene unit was now doing their thing. He'd already gotten a statement from both Hall and Charlotte. Now it was just a matter of trying to figure out their next steps. He saw his friends, now standing against the wall, Charlotte rubbing her boyfriend's back. Charlotte had already told Bradham how hard Hall was taking it, so the detective approached cautiously.

"You really should go to the hospital and get checked out, you know."

"I'm fine," Hall said.

Charlotte looked at Bradham and gave him a sort of face, indicating that he was just wasting his breath.

"It's not your fault, Brandon," Bradham said.

"So everyone keeps saying."

"Please just listen," Charlotte said.

"Brandon, you're a man, not a machine," the detective continued. "You can't run forever on no sleep, no food, no energy. You need rest. There's no shame in falling asleep. It could happen to anybody. This isn't on you. What makes you think if you got in his way first, that he wouldn't have shot and killed you, then moved on to her? Then you both might be dead."

"One's a guess. The other's a sure thing."

"Everything's a guess. I mean, if you want to, you could put this on me. Maybe I didn't do enough here. Maybe I should've stayed. We could go on and on with this for hours, but it wouldn't get us anywhere."

"The fact remains that I was here. And I didn't stop it."

"Listen, all you can do is what you can do. She was also offered protection and refused."

"Don't blame her."

"I'm not blaming her," Bradham said. "But there's only one person who's truly responsible for what happened here, and that's Coulson."

"Two. Ripper."

"One we can prove. The jury is still out on the other."

"You know he's involved."

"Knowing it and proving it are two different things. The only one we can definitely tie in to everything, including the murders, is Coulson. We know he's the one. When it comes to Ripper, we're just speculating."

"This stinks."

"Murder always stinks. There's nothing pleasant about it. And you never feel better about it. If you do, there's something wrong with you." Hall put his head down and nodded, appreciating the words of encouragement, even if he wasn't sure it was doing any good. Bradham put his hand on Hall's shoulder and patted it a few times. "You're a good guy, Brandon. You care. It's tough to ask much more than that. Go home, get some rest."

After a few more minutes of convincing, they finally seemed to get through to Hall, and he decided to go home for the night. They all hoped he would feel better in the morning after he got some rest. As Hall and Charlotte walked to their car, Bradham's phone rang. It was a brief conversation, lasting only a minute or so. After he was done, he started running towards Hall and Charlotte, catching them before they left.

"Hey, we just got an anonymous tip about Coulson being holed up in some apartment about twenty minutes from here."

"Credible?" Hall asked.

"I don't know. I'm about to go find out. What do you say, wanna come with?"

Hall nodded, feeling a little enthusiastic about it, desperately wanting another shot at Coulson. "You bet I do."

"Come on. You guys hop in my car. I'll do the driving."

Hall and Charlotte followed the detective to his car, jumping in the back seat as Bradham put his lights and sirens on. He would turn them off a few minutes before getting to their destination, not wanting to alert Coulson that they were coming.

"What was this tip?" Hall asked.

"I dunno. Just a call that came into dispatch. Said they recognized Coulson's picture from the news. Said he just came into his apartment, cuts on his face, looking all beat up."

"Strange that the call comes in now after this."

"Probably why it did. A man that's all cut up is someone that's easily noticeable. If not for that, they might not have even recognized him."

"Maybe."

Something didn't seem right to Hall. It seemed much too big a coincidence. But for Bradham, it wasn't much of a coincidence at all. That's how they got breaks sometimes. Right after something happened, someone acting strange, someone rushing, someone looking familiar, it happened like that far more than people thought. And anonymous tips? If he was living next to Coulson, he wouldn't want to broadcast his name all over the place either.

Once they got to the apartment complex that Coulson was living in, there was already a big police presence outside. There were police cars blocking off every entrance, only letting authorized personnel in or out. There were a dozen other cops outside, looking up at Coulson's third-floor apartment via the balcony, not that anyone was out there. As soon as Bradham got there, he took control of the situation as the highest-ranking officer on the scene. He was informed of what was going on, then went inside.

Hall and Charlotte followed him up the staircase until he reached the third floor. They were immediately met by another half-dozen police officers, waiting on orders for what to do next.

"People been moved out of these rooms yet?" Bradham asked.

"Yes, sir," an officer replied. "There's nobody left on this floor. We've also cleared out the people above and below this floor. They're in a safe area on the other side of the building."

"Good. Anyone made contact with him yet?"

The officer shook his head. "No. There's no landline phone in there, and we've tried to communicate through the door. No response yet."

"Hear anything? TV, voice, music, another person?"

"Nothing. Quiet as can be."

"Knocked on the door?"

"We've tried everything. He's just not responding."

"OK. Guess we know what to do next," Bradham

Dark Day

said. He then looked to Hall and Charlotte. "You guys stay back."

Hall and Charlotte took a few steps back, standing toward the end of the hallway, far away from the entrance of the door. Bradham went over to the door and knocked, announcing his presence. He waited a few seconds, knowing full well that he wasn't going to get an answer. He then looked to the officer next to him with the battering ram.

"You know what to do."

The officer with the ram stepped in front of the door and broke it open on his third try. Then he stepped aside and let the others go in first, the officers who had shields in front of them to protect them from incoming bullets. There were eight of them that went in. Bradham went in after them. It didn't take long for them to assess the situation, though. It was right there in front of them. Bradham immediately spotted Coulson's body on the floor as the other officers cleared the rest of the apartment. Bradham knelt next to the body and checked the vitals. There were none. Coulson was gone, and with him, the last lead they had to Ripper. There would be no finding Ripper now.

The rest of the apartment was clear, and Bradham stepped out into the hallway, motioning for Hall and Charlotte to come to him. They did, and once they got to the door, the detective pointed inside at the body that was clearly visible from their position.

"Is that him?" Charlotte asked, not seeing his face as clearly as the rest of him.

"Remi Coulson," Bradham answered. "In the flesh."

"What happened?" Hall asked.

Bradham shrugged. "Who knows? There's a bullet in the side of his head and a gun on the floor next to him. Do the math."

"Suicide?"

"That's how it's looking."

"You believe that?"

"You mean, do I actually believe that Ripper came in here, killed his partner to make it look like a suicide, then left? Anything's possible. We'll have to do some interviewing of neighbors and all."

"I bet you won't find the one who made that phone call," Hall said.

Bradham looked at him, his meaning clear. "You mean Ripper."

Hall nodded. "Coulson called him after leaving Candy's apartment, told him what happened, so Ripper said he'd meet him here. Once he arrived, Ripper put a gun to his head, pulled the trigger, then left, calling the police on the way out. Everything all nice and neat."

"And with no other way to trace him," Charlotte said.

Bradham wasn't sure that was the case, but he wouldn't have been surprised either. It was easily possible. But if that was the case, he knew the rest of their investigation was over right then and there. They had nobody else who was connected to Ripper who was alive, so any chance of finding him was remote. They would eventually check out the other building that Hyde told them about, the former pharmacy building, but the chance of them finding anything relevant there was remote as well. The three of them stood there, looking at Coulson's body, realizing that everything was done.

"This just screams Rankin to me," Hall said. "It's the same MO as the last time we were after him. Everyone's dead but him. He ties off all the loose ends, then moves on to something else. And nobody knows anything about him."

"That may be so, but we've still done some good here," Bradham said. "A dangerous killer's off the streets. That's a win in my book."

"But how many innocent people lost their lives in the process?"

"The others involved in that insurance scheme weren't innocent."

"I wasn't talking about them. Candy, Armstrong, Coulson's girlfriend… him checking out wasn't worth the cost."

"It never is. But we've prevented anyone else from going down by his hands."

"Except Rankin," Hall said. "Or Ripper. Whoever he is. He's still out there."

"We'll run into him again. I'm sure of that."

"So am I. I'm gonna find him. If it's the only thing I ever do as a PI, I'm gonna find him. I'll swear to that."

ABOUT THE AUTHOR

Mike Ryan is a USA Today Bestselling Author. He lives in Pennsylvania with his wife, and four children. He's the author of the bestselling Silencer Series, as well as many others. Visit his website at www.mikeryanbooks.com to find out more about his books, and sign up for his newsletter. You can also interact with Mike via Facebook, and Instagram.

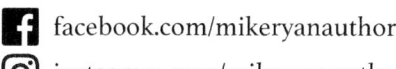

facebook.com/mikeryanauthor
instagram.com/mikeryanauthor

ALSO BY MIKE RYAN

Continue reading the Brandon Hall series with the next book, Loose Ends.

OTHER BOOKS:

The Silencer Series

The Extractor Series

The Cain Series

The Eliminator Series

The Ghost Series

The Cari Porter Series

A Dangerous Man

The Last Job

The Crew

Printed in Great Britain
by Amazon